KINCADE'S EARLY YEARS

Michael Chandler & Loahna Chandler

WAGONMASTER BOOKS

2010

WAGONMASTER
BOOKS

The word "Wagonmaster Books" and the depiction of the Branding Iron logo are trademarks of Wagonmaster Books, a division of TCMC Inc, and are registered with the Colorado Secretary of State.

Library of Congress Control Number: 2009942834

ISBN: 978-0-9841651-1-7

Printed in the United States of America

Published by Wagonmaster Books
A division of TCMC Inc.
826 1/2 Grand Avenue
Suites 10, 11, & 12
Glenwood Springs, Colorado 81601
wagonmasterbooks@sopris.net

TO MY ANGELIC MICHELE

"Just as a young Kincade dreamed of Josephine, a young Michael
dreamed of one day finding you"
- Michael

. . . .

TO WARREN

"Sixty-two years is not long enough"
- Loahna

. . . .

SPECIAL THANKS TO A VERY SPECIAL MAN

His name is Hiram Richardson.

Born amidst the rigors of real working cattle ranches spanning
ten thousand acres, raised as a working cowboy skilled at team roping,
bareback and bull riding, Hiram is a 21st century man carved from the
wonder and folklore of the 1880's. The skills shown with his hands
extended far beyond handling the rough stock on those wild Colorado
lands. He began to draw and paint the life he knew so well, creating
action-filled paintings of the vitality and spirit of the Old West. Hi won
a full scholarship to the American Academy of Art in Chicago and the
Art Center College of Design in California, becoming so skilled that
as of today, his stunning paintings grace the covers of over 650 western
books, including the covers of *Kincade's Early Years, Kincade's Fear and
Kincade's Blood.*

Like Michael Chandler, Hi loves the Old West. Visit with Hiram,
and he'll recall one particular moment at one of Chandler's gunfight
reenactments of the OK Corral battle. "It was a great thrill seeing
Michael fire his pistols from the back of a spinning unbroken horse. As
wild as it was, when the dust settled he was still in the saddle, reins in
hand and calmly dropping six more shells in his revolver. Michael is the
real deal. He puts on a great show and his stories capture the life of a
cowboy. I highly recommend this terrific western novel."

More high praise for *Kincade's Fear* and *Kincade's Blood*...

"Michael is as good as Zane Grey"
- *Pelican Publishing Reader's Review*

"Packed with the requisite violence, horseback adventures, rustling, holdups and other trappings of
the mythic western frontier, Chandler's books should satisfy any fan"
- *John Colson Colorado Mountain News Media*

"An entertaining read and fast-moving adventure tale.
Chandler has a fine narrative talent"
- *American Cowboy Magazine*

"If you like your western heroes to be good, and the bad
guys to be utterly despicable, this one delivers"
- *Historical Novels Review*

"[It] has complexities and levels, twists and turns, but, at its heart,
it's simple. It's about morality and adventure."
- *Glenwood Springs (CO) Post Independent*

"A real Western adventure, where good guys are completely good, bad guys are completely bad,
and the women are all beautiful, strong and fiery"
- *Aspen Times (CO)*

"Something is obviously going right with his career as an author of Western fiction"
- *Sopris Sun (CO)*

"A must-read for every western adventure novel reader
and will someday make a great movie"
- *The Cowboy Chronicle, Single Action Shooting Society*

"Anyone looking to fill the void in their reading preferences since the passing of
Louis L'Amour and Tony Hillerman will enjoy the style and the story"
- *N.J. Ed, Flanders New Jersey*

"A riveting quick read keeping you entertained and emotionally involved"
- *Tom Doroff, Shadows of the West*

"A great book leaving you wanting for more. A+ reading"
- *Christine Hess, Hess Originals*

"A great read that had me wincing, angry, lusty and happy"
- *Verne Terwilliger, Torrance California*

More books by Michael Chandler and Loahna Chandler

Dreamweaving, The Secret To Overwhelming Your Business Competition

The Littlest Cowboy's Christmas with John Denver

Kincade's Blood

Kincade's Fear

Available globally through amazon.com

Coming soon from Wagonmaster Books

Kincade's Death

KINCADE'S EARLY YEARS

PART ONE

CHAPTER 1

AGNES JOHNSON GENTLY dabbed the purple bruises on her sister's cheek with a clean, white cloth soaked in Witch Hazel. "Does he do this every time he comes?" she asked, already knowing the dreaded answer.

Angela winced as the cloth touched her raw skin. She nodded. "But he don't come so often now…not since I look like this." Her huge stomach pouched over the wooden chair, dangling between her thin legs. "Tell me I once was pretty, Agnes. Tell me I didn't always look like a bloated cow." Tears rolled slowly from her blackened eyes, one nearly swollen shut.

"You were the prettiest little thing in town. You will be again once the baby is born." Agnes tightened the lid on the bottle and dropped the cloth on the table. Her little sister was the love of her life. It broke her heart to see her beaten. Not just the wounds her lout of a husband did to her flesh, but because of the cruelty he inflicted to her diminishing love for life. "When did his brutality start, Angela? Has he always done this to you?"

"No – not right off. You remember how gallant Archie was when I first met him at the church social. You were there. We both thought he was so handsome in his uniform. He kissed my hand when we were introduced. He walked me in the moonlight that night." Agnes felt it all seemed an eternity ago. "He took me in his arms, said if I'd marry him he'd buy this ranch not far from the Fort where he was stationed. Said he'd end up being a Cattle King and I'd be his Cattle Queen. Said some folks wanted to sell this ranch real bad. We could move right in. It all sounded pretty wonderful at the time."

"Pretty wonderful? Look at this place," said Agnes. "It's a disaster! This is nothing but a dried mud soddy with an outhouse in the back yard! Near where he was stationed? It must be at least five miles to the Fort." Agnes immediately felt regret saying what she had, as it only made her sister feel worse about herself and the bad decisions she had made with Archibald Logan. She paused, allowing her voice to become softer. She took Angela's callused hand in hers. "I'm older than you. I should have known. This is my fault. I should have seen through his lies."

Angela smiled a slow painful grin. "If I remember correctly, back then you thought Archie was quite a catch. Folks said if I hadn't chased him as hard as I did, you woulda' grabbed him. He's closer to your age than mine."

Agnes dismissed Angela's recollections with a shudder. "If Mama and Papa hadn't died of the influenza, they'd have made you wait. It would have given you time to know him better... know the trouble he'd be." Agnes shook her head in dismay over the bleak situation now enveloping them both. "Oh, my dearest little sister, you've been my responsibility. I should have stopped you myself." She sighed and was silent for a minute as Angela wept softly. She felt so sorry for the girl. "Why haven't you left him?"

"Where would I go?"

"Back home to live with me, of course."

Reaching over to the table, Angela took the Witch Hazel rag to wipe her nose. "I couldn't burden you with a useless sister and

KINCADE'S EARLY YEARS   11

her new baby. You have a hard enough time making a living as a midwife without two more mouths to feed."

"You're my little sister. I love you."

She sighed. "Well, what's done is done." The baby kicked and a small wave on Angela's ragged dress lifted and fell. "I'm so glad you're here, Agnes." There was a tremble in her voice. "My time is real soon. I'm scared."

"You should have written me to come sooner."

"Please don't say that again. My life is filled with all the things I 'should have done' or 'could have done'. I know what horrible mistakes I've made. I've married a monster! I wish I'd die having Archie's baby..." Angela burst into tears.

"There, there, little one. You don't mean that." Agnes took her sister in her arms. "I'm here now. Somehow we'll have this baby. Then you can get back to being pretty again."

"I don't want to be pretty. It just makes him have his way with me over and over again." Angela choked. "I used to try to fight him off but he's a big, mean man. I've finally learned to crumple up and lie still so all his fun of attacking me is gone. But it don't help. He just starts drinking and knocking me around." She could hardly talk between sobs. "Look at my face. Look at my black and blue arms where he grabbed me. Look at my back. He whipped me with his riding crop. Agnes, he was here over three days ago. The gashes are still bleeding!"

Agnes dreaded to ask. But this was her sister. She had to know. As gently as she could, Agnes said, "He surely doesn't rape you when you're this far along, does he dear?"

Angela closed her eyes in shame, turning her head away. But after a moment, she nodded. Agnes felt an emptiness envelop her.

Angela's voice became a whisper. "He doesn't want to look at me, to see the hatred in my eyes." A pause from a voice softer still. "He takes me from behind."

Agnes shuddered. She rocked her little sister back and forth without saying anything. If Archie Logan came again while she was here, she swore she would kill him.

Swore to God.

CHAPTER 2

DESPITE THEIR SEEMINGLY hopeless situation, Agnes decided to attack and conquer what she could. Her battlefield was the filth of the soddy and the disaster of the yard that pressed in upon it. Her sister's final weeks of pregnancy had made any work too strenuous, so Agnes put her back into the job.

The one-room soddy regurgitated a cloud of dust as Agnes vigorously swept the dirt floor. Cobwebs gave up their silken holds on dark corners as spiders fled for safe harbor. Cleaning rags, soon choked with grime, were washed and rewashed. Although the earthen walls and floor fought back with a vengeance, a semblance of tidiness appeared. Agnes washed the gray bed linens and spread them over bushes to bleach in the sun.

Turning to the small garden Angela had eked from the soil, Agnes found a few beleaguered vegetables fighting for survival. She harvested what she could, and took those into a poor excuse for a root cellar.

Agnes then scoured the creek hollow, salvaging scraps of debris which she then fashioned into a makeshift corral. Once done, she hoisted herself up and onto the earthen roof of the soddy. There, three goats that Archie had undoubtedly stolen from the army post had taken up residence, obviously enjoying their rooftop views. Agnes shooed them to the ground, bunching them into the corral. Their floppy ears looked twice as forlorn as they surveyed their new home.

Angela watched in silence, seated on a stool in the yard. Her hands were folded on top of her bulbous stomach. Her only smile came when her sister succeeded in booting the goats from their lookout. "You work too hard," was all she could say. She deeply appreciated the care her sister was giving her.

Agnes looked up from gathering eggs from nests under the porch, pleased that the silence was broken. "You're absolutely right. Let's go for a ride in my buggy and talk about happy things. Would you like that?"

Angela shrugged. "You'll have to help me get in. I must weigh more than a ton."

Seizing the chance for any hope of gaiety, Agnes answered, "Not quite – but almost." They both smiled. Agnes placed the eggs inside the door to the soddy and returned to the yard, kneeling before her sister. "Dearest, it's so good to hear something besides sobbing. Tell you what. I'll hitch up my horse, and give you a big boost into the buggy."

Angela's brow furrowed. "We mustn't go very far. This baby is kicking like it wants to take a ride of its own – downhill."

Agnes nodded. "We'll just take a spin to the main road - a bit of relaxation in this wonderful sunshine. It'll do us both good."

And good it was. It had been a long time since Angela felt so lighthearted, almost like she had been when the two of them were young girls. They bounced along the rutted lane, admiring the sunflowers that lifted their golden heads on each side of the road, and snickering at the raspy scolding of a crow which had to fly out of their path.

Quite suddenly Angela gasped. She reached forward and felt beneath the fabric. "Agnes! My legs are all wet. It's not pee!" She turned white. "Oh no! I don't want to have the baby on the road-side!"

Agnes gave the horse a firm command and the reins a sharp snap. The buggy turned and they sped back to the house. "Don't you worry, dearest. I've made everything ready. The oil cloth is already in place to protect your bed. You'll be resting on it in plenty of time."

With great effort Agnes lifted Angela from the buggy and helped her inside. She folded back the bed covers just as Angela let out her first scream.

"Lie down, dear. Let me prop your head up." Agnes knew exactly what she was doing. Years of midwife practice quickly came into play. "I'm going to pull off your skirt and petticoat. Everything will go smoothly just like I explained. You'll be a mama before this day is through." She smiled at the anxious girl.

"Can you put the sheet over me so I won't feel so naked?"

"Of course." Agnes soothed her baby sister, understanding how frightening all this seemed. She lit the fire in the iron stove, placing the kettle of water on to boil. She got clean cloths from her satchel and arranged them on the table alongside sharp scissors which she dipped in the water when it finally bubbled.

Angela was breathing hard, issuing sharp cries of pain at about four minute intervals. "I didn't know it would hurt this much."

Agnes thought, "It's going to get worse before it gets any better." But she just held her sister's hand and said reassuringly, "Every one on this whole earth came into the world in this same way. If hundreds and thousands of women can do it, so can you."

Angela let out a terrified shriek. "Am I going to die, Agnes? If I'm dying please hold me in your arms – tight." She gave an even more agonizing wail.

"No, dearest. You're not going to die. I won't let you. But come into my arms anyhow." She lifted Angela's shoulders to enfold the quivering girl in a motherly embrace. "Try to breathe deeply and begin to push gently."

They stayed this way for almost two hours. The contractions became more constant and Angela's screams more piercing. Agnes had delivered many babies in her ten years as midwife but none as distressing to watch as the delivery of this unwanted child. Her arms ached in the cramped position. But if her little sister received any comfort from being held she would continue as long as it took. "Dear God," she mumbled. "Lessen her suffering – let this not continue beyond endurance."

Agnes put Angela's head back on the pillow. "Let me take a peek at the progress." She lifted the bloody sheet and spread Angela's legs to their fullest. She was relieved when she saw the head in position.

Agnes left the bedside and washed her hands with very hot water and strong soap. "Angela, it's time to really go to work. No more fooling around. Those pushes have got to be stronger. Do you understand?"

Angela nodded. Sweat poured over her entire body. With a shattering groan she forced her stomach to press against the little body struggling inside her.

Agnes pulled the sheet off the bed. "Good. Another one. Good. Another just like before. Good." She extended her hands. "There! I can grasp the head. Keep pushing. Here come the shoulders. Good! It's over!"

A slap on the behind and the newborn took its first gulp of air, expelling fluid from its mouth and replacing it with a cry that was not unlike the yipping of a coyote. "Did you hear that, Angela? His first word was Mama." Agnes beamed. "You have a baby boy, Angela!" She patted the child and continued to encourage its small but healthy cries.

Angela was too exhausted to care. She wanted only to slip away from any more pain.

Agnes quickly took the baby to the folded cloths on the table and cut the umbilical cord. She carefully began to sponge away the birth film and clean out the tiny nose. She then wrapped the child and placed it in the cradle which had been left behind by the former owners of the small soddy. Then she turned to attend once again to her sister who lay wide-eyed and breathing hard.

"Something's wrong, Agnes. My pains are more severe than ever." She grabbed her sister's hand as she yelled, "God have mercy! I can bear no more! Let me die!"

"Hush, Angela. You'll be all right. Let me look." Agnes spread the legs again and pushed her fingers up into the blood and pain.

She had seen this happen a few times before. Angela's trial of birth was only half over. There was a twin pushing to be born.

She waited a half hour surrounded by the screams of her beloved sister. "Dearest, I must examine you again." What she saw put a chill up her spine. There was not a head in the passageway, but a tiny buttock. This twin was breech. Agnes remembered the tragedy of many years ago when she had tried to deliver another breech child. That baby had died, along with its mother. "I will not let that happen now," she silently vowed.

She took Angela's hand and stroked the white, trembling fingers. "The twin is coming out backwards. I will have to turn it before it can pass."

"Kill it! Kill it!" Angela screamed. "Cut it into little pieces so you can pull it out. I can stand no more!"

Agnes looked around the room. "Where is Archie's whiskey?"

Angela nodded to a cupboard near the door. Agnes found the half-empty bottle and poured the remainder in a cup. "Drink this," she ordered. "It might help. I'm not going to kill this child."

"Even if it is killing me?" Her voice was hysterical.

"Drink it! – All of it!"

Angela emptied the cup and fell back on the bed, too helpless to argue. Perhaps she could die soon and it would be over.

The sun crested over the eastern horizon when Angela's eyes finally fluttered. She looked at her tired but happy sister who had held her hand hour after hour while she wore off the drugged sleep. "Did the baby live?" she asked in a horse whisper.

"Yes, and so did you. You have twin sons, Angela."

"Where are they?"

"One's in the cradle and the other in the big laundry basket. Shall I bring them to you?" She nodded. Agnes placed one on each side of their mother. "This one is the older. I think he looks like you." Angela smiled at the tiny but well formed infant. His mouth formed little movements as if he were remembering a happy dream.

Agnes continued. "This one put up quite a fight to stay where he was, but I finally won."

"Do you think he looks like Archie?"

Agnes stared at the red wrinkles of a battered baby. A scowl settled on the puckered face as if coming into this world was not his idea. "It's been a long time since I've seen Archie." She paused. "Do you feel up to nursing?"

"I'm ready if they are. Which one first, or do they each get a breast?"

Agnes laughed. "You have a lot to learn, little Mother. Let's give the older one his first breakfast." Angela bared her breast and Agnes laid the baby alongside. She picked up the younger and put him back in the basket. He began yelling much louder than she thought possible for a new-born. "Hush, little boy. Your turn's coming."

She went back to watch Angela who had a smile across her face that suited her name. "He's pretty cute, don't you think?" the proud mother asked as he gently suckled. "Who taught him to do that?"

Agnes shrugged. "Sometimes there are hints that we should believe in God...."

The baby boy in the basket began his insistent cry again. The six words that suddenly entered Agnes' mind startled her, so much so that her brow furrowed. She kept the words to herself.

"...and also believe in the Devil."

CHAPTER 3

FOUR WEEKS PASSED. Archibald Logan still had not come to see his sons. "He's probably waiting for me to leave," Agnes commented to Angela, and she added to herself, "Smart man, considering how I detest him."

The new mother lifted one child from her breast and put him in Agnes's arms. She took the other from the laundry basket. Angela sighed as he began his turn to suckle. She cringed a little. "They are so different. Johnson there," and she pointed to the baby in her sister's arms, "is gentle and I feel the warmth flowing between us. But Sherwood here," and she nodded at the child at her breast, "is more intent on biting me than getting his milk. I am really quite sore."

"We can fashion a bottle from a rabbit skin and fill it with goat's milk if you'd prefer."

Angela grinned mischievously. "Or maybe I'll just let him suckle the Nanny." Her sense of humor had returned.

"Nanny might give him a swift kick if he bit her." And they both giggled at their naughty suggestion. "Look at them, Angela – two peas from your pod and their daddy hasn't given them a glance. I'll go home and then he'll pay his family a visit."

Angela looked startled. "Go home? So soon? I was hoping you'd stay forever."

"Actually I've been planning to leave for some time. I just didn't know how to break the news. I have patients at home anxiously awaiting my return before their delivery time." She put the baby into his cradle. "You're strong enough now to care for yourself and the babies without me."

"Not really. I need you, Agnes."

"No, you want me – not need me, and that's nice to know." She looked with compassion into her sister's eyes, seeing the unpleasant future she'd probably endure. "Why don't you come live with me? I'd love having you and the babies."

Angela wanted to jump at this pleasant offer, but she knew it wouldn't work. "Archie'd only come looking for me. As long as he lives I'm his property. He's told me that often enough."

"He'll beat you again, you know."

"Maybe not. Maybe he'll be right proud of these two boys I gave him. Maybe he'll be nicer to me now." She said this so Agnes wouldn't worry, but she really didn't believe it.

She put the sleepy baby down and covered his bald head. "When will you go?"

"I'll be on my way after breakfast tomorrow." Angela started to cry. "None of that now. We'll keep in touch. He does bring you the mail from the Fort, doesn't he?" She nodded. "And I'll send you baby clothes that have been outgrown by my former newborns. How's that sound?"

"You're an angel, Agnes."

"No, you are the Angela – I'm just old Auntie Agnes."

True to Agnes's prediction, Archie arrived at the ranch to see his sons the day after she left. He and two men of his platoon arrived at a gallop. Dismounting in a whirl of dust, Archie kicked open the cabin door with the heel of his big riding boot. The men followed him inside.

"So where are they, Angie? I didn't ride all this way just to see you." He looked her up and down. "But you are looking considerably better."

She pointed to the cradle. "This here one is Johnson. I named him for my father." Then she pointed to the laundry basket. "And this one is Sherwood, my mother's maiden name."

Archie's glance showed no reaction except disgust. "You got no right to name my sons after your pa and ma. They only whelped two puking girls, but I begat sons and I'll give them the names I choose." He looked from one to the other baby. "Which was born first?" Angela pointed to the cradle.

"Then he's named after my First Lieutenant – Kincade." He turned to his companion. "How you like that, soldier?"

"Thanks, Captain. I always wanted a kid named for me."

Archie picked up the second baby and held it high. "And this little fellow is named for you, Sergeant – Wilson."

"Much obliged, Captain." He touched the bill of his army cap.

Angela reached for the child but Archie tossed the baby in the air, pretending to almost miss the catch when the infant came down. He laughed just as the newly-christened Wilson threw up milk all over his freshly cleaned military jacket.

"God damn!" Archie yelled as he thrust the baby into Angela's outstretched hands. He stared at the puke and then slapped the infant hard across the mouth. "That'll teach you to spit on your pappy!"

"Archie! How could you! He's only a baby!" Angela clutched the screaming child to her breast.

"Maybe you deserve the same treatment." Angela backed away as Archie was unbuttoning his jacket. "Clean off this vomit. And change their dydees. This room smells like a shit house. I'll wait outside."

As Angela hurried to obey his orders, she heard the three talking while they rolled and smoked cigarettes. The two soldiers were bragging about their names being bestowed on the Captain's off-spring. All were laughing at the names Johnson and Sherwood. "Sound like a sissy woman's choice – her parents. God, how stupid can she be!"

Angela brought the clean jacket to the porch and handed it to Archie. "You'll be on your way now?" she asked hopefully.

He looked at her flat stomach and full breasts. "Not quite yet. Excuse me, fellows. I've one more thing to take care of." He dragged Angela into the soddy and threw her on the bed. In a matter of seconds her flimsy dress was hiked and he was into her, pumping and groaning with pleasure.

She bit her lip to keep from crying out as his roughness penetrated her tender membrane – still bloody from the delivery. Although his grinning face was close to hers, she silently swore, "I will not give him the satisfaction of knowing how I hurt." She kept repeating this in her mind. "At least I won't get pregnant again from what Agnes told me. Some good came from that long night of torture."

Archie was finished and pulled up his britches, stretching the black suspenders over his broad shoulders. "See you soon, Sweetheart. And don't forget the names of my boys – Kincade and Wilson. You got that?"

She nodded. But she thought, "I'll call the little darling Kincade. But I'll never call the other boy 'son'. I'll call him Wil if I must - but never Wilson – Archie's son."

CHAPTER 4

A NGELA WOULD LOOK back on the first six months of motherhood as an easy time. All she had to do was draw water from the well and haul it to the house for drinking and cooking. She did the washing outside on a work bench. This was a daily chore since she had only four dydees until the package arrived from Agnes with a dozen more as well as infant garments. Winter was coming so Angela gathered fallen trees and sawed them into lengths, stacking the wood against the south wall. She split kindling which was kept in a large wooden box. There was a garden to hoe, traps to check for animals which needed to be skinned and dressed for cooking, apples to be gathered beneath the three trees and then stored in a barrel in the root cellar. She tried to deal with the rodents which invaded all the storage places as well as the cabin. She had such poor luck trying to smack them with a shovel that she finally asked Archie to bring her some poison.

The babies slept quietly through all her bustling around unless they were hungry. Then when one awoke crying for her breast, the other was sure to open his eyes and join in the demand. Angela looked forward to the cessation of work, to sit rocking and singing what she liked to call The Happy Song. "Mother didn't have any little boys; poor lonesome Mother; Mother said to God, please send me two little boys; the sweetest ones you have in heaven.

God sent Mother her own Kincade and Wil – eensie, weensie, teensie, tiny babies. But those babies will grow and grow until they are great big boys."

Kincade loved The Happy Song and snuggled down into his mother's arms. Wil's eyes looked up at her with baby anger. "Why did you feed him first?" they seemed to say. Or if she picked him up before Kincade he glared, "Don't rush me. I never get enough." Angela told herself she only imagined these thoughts from her tiny son. But why should she even imagine them unless they were put in her mind by some filial vibration? She would kiss the top of Wil's head to assure him that her love was equal, but she would immediately put him back in the laundry basket and not rock him after the feeding as she did Kincade.

Archie was not a frequent visitor. When he finally did come he just stared at his sleeping sons. "Are they wet?" he asked.

Angela shook her head. "I just changed them. Would you like to hold Kincade or Wil?" She made a point of shortening the name.

"He's Wilson," Archie emphatically corrected her. "And no, I don't want to hold either."

"I've made a list of a few things we need here." She handed him a slip of paper. "Would you please get them for me?"

Archie read the list, "Hmm. Beans, flour, coffee, salt, corn meal….." He put the list in his pocket. "I'll send an orderly with them in a day or two."

"Also any letter or box from Agnes - should one have arrived," she added with great apprehension.

"What am I? A delivery service?"

"Please, Archie." Her smile was coy.

"Well, I'll be damned. For a moment there you looked like the pretty little thing I married." He pulled her close. "And not the ugly, stinking slut you've become." He tore open her blouse and grabbed her swollen breast with one hand as he pulled down his suspenders with the other.

The twins were awakened by his loud voice and immediately started to cry. Angela pulled away. "Please, Archie. They'll just keep that up until I feed them."

As he unbuttoned his pants he looked at her milk-full mammas. "First come, first served." And he lowered his lips over her right nipple and sucked hard. He quickly spit onto the floor. "God, that tastes terrible. I can get better milk from a magpie." He swished saliva around in his mouth and spit again. "Are you trying to kill my sons?"

Angela broke from his hold and went to the cradle, lifting Kincade. "Get out, Archie. I've got better things to do than listen to you."

"And I've got better tits to suck in the whore house." He pulled up his suspenders and buttoned his pants. "Don't expect to see those vittles you want, Angie – not for a long, long time – maybe never!" He strode out of the door, jumped on his horse, and galloped away with the speed of a dust devil.

Angela sang The Happy Song and nursed Kincade while Wil continued to cry in the laundry basket.

CHAPTER 5

BY THE TIME the twins were seven months they could sit up. By eight months they could crawl, and Angela's life became considerably harder. No matter what she was doing she had to keep one eye on Wil. She feared for his safety since he frequently headed for the hot stove or open door. Kincade would be content playing with whatever three things she placed before him – three spoons, three little boxes, three clothes pins. Outside both would sit in the dirt while their mother did the chores. Kincade would play with a daisy chain she'd made for him. Wil would find worms or bugs to eat which usually made him throw up. Angela would scold him as she washed out his mouth with soap but he didn't seem to care and the next time outside he'd be eating them again.

By ten months the boys were pulling themselves to their feet by hanging onto chairs and tables and bedding. Kincade carefully tested his legs and then usually settled back down again to crawl. Wil tried to tip over the chair, or sweep something off the table, or pull the blanket to the floor. More often than she realized, Angela was saying, "Oh, Wil! Why can't you be a good boy like Kincade?"

The boys had long outgrown the cradle and laundry basket. They now slept with their mother in the only bed. Angela had pushed it against the wall so neither could fall out that side and she slept facing the room. A boy's reward for being good all day was to sleep next to Mama, the naughty child being bedded next to the wall. Wil was given this spot more often than not and he would kick the wall until Angela said, "Wil, be quiet like your brother!"

Angela gave no thought to her age, let alone when her birthday occurred, until a box wrapped in heavy brown paper arrived from Agnes. The enclosed note read: Happy Nineteenth Birthday, dear sister. I know there is nothing I could buy you that would mean as much as this childhood treasure. Remember how we used to dance around to the music? I love you. Agnes.

Carefully Angela unwrapped all the packing and pulled out the lovely, little music box with the dancing couple on top that her mama and papa had given her on her ninth birthday. All the memories of a happy family flooded back and her heart beat with joy to have her precious bauble again.

She wound the key and as the Strauss waltz played, the tiny couple twirled around the miniature dance floor. Angela clapped her hands. "Come, come, boys. See the pretty thing that Auntie Agnes sent me." She scooped up one under each arm and placed them on her lap at the table. "Watch and listen. Isn't that wonderful?"

Wil looked at the music box with no surprise or delight. He slipped to the floor and started tearing the brown wrapping paper into little pieces. Kincade kept his eyes pealed on the dancers, his head cocked to listen. He laughed and clapped his hands to the music. Angela was delighted. "May I have this dance, Kincade?" She scooped him up in her arms and began waltzing around the room.

Wil watched with a sour look on his face. Then very quietly he pulled himself up to the table. Angela heard a crash and stopped dancing. Wil had pushed the music box to the floor and it lay in a broken mess of glass and wires and metal disk. The dancers were separated, faces down. She dropped Kincade and burst into deep sobs. "Oh, you monster son! You just destroyed the only happiness I've had since you were born! Get in bed! Turn your face to the wall! You'll stay there forever if I have my way!" She sank into a chair, shaking with grief as Wil went where she pointed.

Kincade put his arms around his mother's legs and his head on her lap. He said nothing, but his understanding touch meant everything.

That Christmas Archie brought his sons a bag of wooden blocks of different shapes and sizes. "Kincade's are square and Wilson's are round," he told them. He spilled the blocks on the floor and both boys began sorting them.

He also brought Angela a new flowered cotton dress. "Thank you," she said without smiling.

"Aren't you going to put it on for me?"

"If you want me to." She pulled her worn Mother Hubbard over her head and stood in her chemise.

Archie looked her up and down. "You can put it on later." He pulled her towards the bed.

"Please, Archie, not in front of the boys."

"Shut up! They're busy with their blocks. They don't care what we're doing."

Later that afternoon, while Kincade was building a tower with his blocks, Wil was behind the big rocker, straddling a pillow, pushing and groaning as he'd seen and heard his father do. When Angela found him she jerked out the pillow. "You're a naughty, naughty boy!" He looked at her without understanding. "Where are your blocks? Go play nice with them like Kincade does."

At dinner time, when she went to the kindling box to start the fire in the stove, she found the round blocks. "Wil! Have you thrown away your papa's nice Christmas gift? You're an ungrateful, very bad boy! Look at the wall Kincade is building with his blocks." He stared at her with wide eyes. "Go!" She pointed to the bed. "You get no supper tonight!"

Wil lay on the far side of the bed with his face against the wall. He wasn't sure why he'd made his mother mad. But he wore a grin just the same.

CHAPTER 6

BOTH KINCADE AND Wil began walking at thirteen months and were steady on their feet by a year and a half. Kincade followed Angela everywhere and tried to help her in his own small way. He would hand her the clothes pins as she hung washing on the line and drop them into a bag when she took the dry laundry down. He carried the wood she chopped and he stacked it by the side of the house or dropped into the barrel of kindling. When Angela milked the goats, she half-filled a small bucket which he took into the house for her. She showed him how to carefully carry dishes from the table to the sink. He always put away any toys, both his and Wil's, before bed. He did these things and many more with a cheery smile and she paid him for each effort with a hug.

Wil, on the other hand, made work for his mother. He drowned newborn kittens in the trough where the goats drank, and Angela buried them with Kincade's help. Angela knew he'd break her dishes if he helped clear the table so she only trusted him with the metal tableware which he deliberately dropped. One time he ran back and forth under a sheet on the clothes line until it fell to the ground. He put it over his head and ran around the yard trailing it behind him. Angela stomped her foot and shook him. "Naughty boy! I'll have to wash it again! Why can't you be helpful like Kincade?" She wanted to give him a good spanking, but the one time she had done so, he retaliated by being more naughty than ever. "What shall I do with that boy?" She kept asking herself. "What he needs is a stern father!" But she didn't want Archie to come because disciplining Wil would be the last thing on his mind.

By the time the twins were two their childish gibberish was sounding like words. They clearly could say, "I'm Kincade" and "I'm Wil". Angela wanted them to say "please" and "thank you", and Kincade learned to do so immediately. But Wil didn't use these courtesies correctly. If she scolded him, he would say, "Thank you, Mama." And if she threatened him with going to bed without any supper he'd say, "Please, Mama." His grin always showed that he knew he was aggravating his mother which gave him much pleasure.

Agnes sent Angela clothes for the growing boys and once she enclosed a children's book with many drawings. Kincade and his mother would sit on the porch while she read and pointed out the toys, and animals, and funny people on the colorful pages. He would repeat each word after her. His vocabulary grew rapidly, and soon he could tell her each word printed under the pictures.

Angela worried that she didn't encourage this learning with her other son. "Come sit with us, Wil. You'll like this book as much as Kincade does. It has pretty pictures." But the stubborn boy would stick out his tongue at her and run in the opposite direction.

Angela sighed and returned to reading. After the lesson she put her arm around Kincade and sang a new verse of The Happy Song. "Mother isn't lonesome any more, now that she has Kincade. For Kincade is smart, and Kincade can read. I guess I ought to know." Wil was within earshot and he heard and understood. He kicked the dirt with his bare foot and then picked up some rocks to throw at the chickens.

The next year deepened the personalities of the twin boys. She sometimes wondered if they had sprung from two very different bloodlines. Kincade was all things good – helpful, intelligent, creative, appreciative, loving. Wil was all things bad – obstinate, boorish, resentful, vengeful, cruel. "Where did these traits come from?" Angela asked herself. And she concluded they were inherited from the only bad person she had ever known in her life – Archibald Logan.

Then something happened which showed a side of Kincade that Angela had never seen before – defiance against cruelty.

When Archie arrived Angela was sitting on the porch chair shelling peas while Kincade and Wil played at her feet with the discarded pods. He slipped from his horse, strode up the steps, and jerked her to her feet. The bowl of peas spilled from her lap. "I have need of you, wife."

"Please, Archie. I can't leave the boys outside alone."

"The hell you can't. Get in the house."

Wil began eating the scattered peas while Kincade was putting them back in the bowl. When their parents emerged they were fighting because Wil couldn't find any more to eat and Kincade wouldn't give him any in the bowl.

Archie laughed. "It's a boy thing. Go at it with your fists, fellas."

"Do no such thing!" Angela took the bowl with one hand and separated the boys with the other. She turned to Archie. "Maybe you could play with your sons a little bit before you go." He looked at the boys who were staring at him wide-eyed, thinking this man only played with their Mama.

"Sure." He sat in the porch chair. Kincade started toward him but Wil pushed him aside. He pointed to himself and said, "Me first."

Archie laughed. "Whatever you say, little man. Papa's going to give you a horsie ride." He lifted Wil to straddle his right knee and, holding onto his hands, he began to gently move him up and down.

"This is the way the ladies ride, the ladies ride, the ladies ride." Wil smiled at his father. "This is the way the ladies ride, so early in the morning."

Archie began to bounce Wil faster. "This is the way the gentlemen ride, the gentlemen ride, the gentlemen ride." Wil began to chortle with glee. "This is the way the gentlemen ride, so early in the morning."

Now Archie violently lifted and lowered his knee as fast as he could, tossing Wil up into the air. "This is the way the soldiers ride…."

"Be more careful!" Angela shouted.

"Shut up, woman!" He laughed with the boy who had never had so much fun. "…the soldiers ride, the soldiers ride." Wil was cheering in his childish voice. "This is the way the soldiers ride, so early in the morning."

Archie gave an extremely high knee lift and Wil pulled his hands free of his father's grip. The boy fell over backwards, landing on the porch with a terrible thump, knocking his head against the post. He lay there, perfectly still, his eyes closed.

"My God, Archie! You've killed your own son!" Angela rushed to pick up her baby but Archie pushed her back.

"Nonsense. He's just playing possum." He slapped Wil hard on both cheeks. "Wake up, you little brat. You're not hurt."

Wil slowly opened his eyes and looked around. When he saw

his mother he held out his arms. "Please Mama." He began to cry. She fell to her knees and tried to reach him.

Archie kicked her. "Oh no you don't. It's time he learned a soldier's lesson."

He looked fiercely at Wil. "Stand up!" Wil just lay there. "I said stand up! Obey your commanding officer!"

"Archie, please. He's just a little boy."

"Shut up!"

Wil got to a crawling position but Archie pulled him to his feet by the back of his collar. "Stand at attention and listen to your Captain." Wil sniffed back tears.

"When a soldier falls he doesn't just lie on his back and call for his mama. He gets up and gets back on his horse. And you're going to do the same."

Archie started to lift Wil back onto his knee but this time Angela grabbed her son first. "Oh, no you don't. He's had enough of you for one day." She held him tight against her body.

Archie laughed. "A Mama's Boy, huh?" Wil broke free from her embrace and ran into the house, crying.

Archie then turned to Kincade who had been watching without saying a word. "What about you, little man?" He grabbed Kincade's arm. "Are you going to be a better soldier than your brother?"

Kincade climbed onto his father's knee with absolute loathing in his eyes.

Archie started the gentle bouncing. "This is the way the ladies ride, the ladies ride, the ladies ride…" There was not a childish smile this time, only an intense unblinking stare into Archie's eyes.

"This is the way the gentlemen ride…." Kincade scowled harder. Archie pinched Kincade's cheeks together between his fingers. "Smile, damn it!" The boy clenched his teeth.

"This is the way the soldiers ride…." Archie began to jounce Kincade harder and higher than he had Wil. But this son grabbed his father's hair with both hands and pulled as hard as he could.

"You son of a bitch!" Archie jumped up, throwing Kincade to the floor. The boy slammed into the wall, knocking the breath from his lungs. As he gasped for air, Kincade looked directly at Archie and smiled ever so slightly.

Archie stomped to his horse, swung up without touching the stirrups. "I mean what I said, Angie – you're a bitch and that makes him a son-of-a-bitch." He rode off in a swirl of dust.

Angela sat on the porch step with her arm around Kincade's shoulder. She sang softly, "Mother didn't have any little boy; poor lonesome Mother. Mother said to God please send me a little boy; the bravest one you have in heaven. God sent Mother her own Kincade…."

Wil stood in the doorway listening. Angela never saw the look of hatred on his tear-stained face… but this hatred extended to everyone and everything.

"Someday, somehow," thought little Wil Logan, "I'll get them all…"

CHAPTER 7

ARCHIE HADN'T COME for almost a year. When he galloped into the yard she hardly recognized him. He'd grown a beard which was streaked with gray. His uniform was dirty and wrinkled. As he swung down from his horse he staggered and almost fell. He was obviously drunk.

Angela stood on the porch with her hands on her hips. "What do you want?" Her tone was not welcoming.

"Just a little understanding and sympathy from my family." His words were slurred.

"You've come to the wrong place." As he came towards her she noticed that, although he still wore an officer's uniform, the Captain's insignia was no longer on the shoulder loops and he didn't wear his officer's cap. He pushed past her. "Let me in, Angie."

Kincade was seated at the table, using crayons that Agnes had sent to put colors on a book of animal drawings. He didn't know this stranger was his father, and he had grown so much that Archie didn't recognize him.

"Hello, Wilson. What you doing?"

"I'm Kincade." He kept on drawing, not liking the foul breath that leaned over him.

Archie grabbed the coloring book. "I said what you doing, Wilson?"

Kincade's eyes flashed. "I said, I'm Kincade."

"Now how could I have made that mistake – not to know my own son?"

"You don't look like my papa. I don't know who you are."

"You don't know I'm Archibald Logan and you're Kincade Logan?" Archie whipped out a knife from his pocket and snapped the switchblade open. "I'll make sure that never happens again!"

Kincade was wearing coveralls without any shirt. Archie grabbed the bare right arm and held it tight. "I'll put my mark on you and then you'll never again forget that you're Kincade Logan!"

To Angela's horror, the sharp knife cut into the tender skin. "That's a "K", in case you can't read yet." Blood spurted from the gash. Angela was too shocked to move. "And this here's an "L" – for Logan."

Angela lunged for the knife which was just about to make the horizontal slash of the 'L'. "My God, Archie! Have you gone crazy?! He's just a little boy!" She looked around for something to staunch the bright red flow. Kincade was too bewildered to immediately react. He stared at his arm and then whimpered, "Mama?"

"Get out, you maniac. Get away from my son!" The door slammed behind him. She tore a strip from her petticoat and was wrapping the arm when she heard Archie's voice in the yard.

"Wilson, come here boy. Where are you?"

The four year old stepped boldly from behind the wood pile. "I'm Wil. Who are you?"

"I'm your papa, and just so you'll never forget…." He grabbed the bare arm just like he had in the house. The open switchblade still had Kincade's blood on it. The knife zigzagged across the small bicep. "That's a "W" – for WILSON – not Wil…and.." The blade began its downward slash. "And this here's the "L" for Logan." He dug deeper. "Remember who your papa…"

Angela had suddenly realized that her other son was in equal danger. She bolted from the house in time to stop the knife half way through the carving of the 'L'.

"You're a mad man! What right have you to mutilate your own sons?" Wil was screaming and she held his arm to her breast, trying to stop the flow from the wound with her blouse.

"I've every right." He staggered, brandishing the knife. "They're my property, and you're my property, and I'll do whatever I goddamn want with all three of you."

He threw Wil to one side and grabbed Angela, ripping open her blouse. "Two down, one to go." She saw the knife swinging back and forth in front of her eyes. Then she fainted.

When Angela gained consciousness the boys were sobbing over her and calling, "Mama, Mama, wake up." She blinked her eyes to focus. What she saw was almost enough to make her pass out again. Their arms were covered with blood which had dripped onto their overalls in wide, red streaks. But the blood wasn't coming just from the boys' injuries. It was coming from hers.

Angela looked down at her chest and saw it covered in blood. There, just above her breasts were carved the initials 'A' and 'L'. Archibald Logan had branded all three of them.

How long had she been unconscious? She had no idea. The butcher of a husband was nowhere to be seen. Angela sat up. "Help me stand," she said to both her sons, for she felt quite faint again. Kincade and Wil each took an arm and helped her to her feet. With a voice as brave as she could muster, she spoke. "Come, darlings. I'll clean us up."

Angela found some of the dydees she had put away after the boys were toilet trained. They were soft and clean. She cut them into lengths. Somewhere there was Witch Hazel that Agnes had used long ago. She found the soothing ointment and bound their arms. The boys had stopped crying and their blood was coagulating. She looked at her own slashes. Blood still dripped down towards her waist. There was no way to hold a bandage so she used the ointment and tightly buttoned her blouse.

What if she had bled to death there in the yard? What would the twins have done if Archie had vanished into the night? Although she could get provoked and impatient with Wil and wish he were more like Kincade, they were both her babies and neither deserved Archie's cruelty. No one did.

The boys were both quiet, looking at their mother for some kind of reassurance. Angela took their hands and led them to the porch. She sat down with one on each side and put her arms around them. She began singing: "Mother didn't have any little boys. Poor lonesome Mother. Mother said to God; please send me two little boys; the sweetest ones you have in heaven. God sent Mother Kincade and Wil…."

That night Angela lay awake in the middle of the bed, hugging both her sons, one on each side of her trembling body.

CHAPTER 8

THE SCARS ON their bodies had healed without infection. But they looked like large red snakes crawling under the skin and were constant reminders of the man who had inflicted them. "I will see Archie in hell before I have anything to do with him ever again!" Angela wrote to Agnes, and her sister replied, "I made that vow long before you did."

This did not mean that Angela refused to accept the groceries and mail which were still brought every month by a Fort orderly. He was a dear boy named Harry. Harry showed her respect, spending some time talking and listening, each time he visited. He accepted a cup of coffee while he told Angela of local happenings and she shared her concerns about Wil. She did not ask him about her husband and he volunteered no such information. She presumed that her husband paid for the groceries, for she never had any money.

One piece of news that Harry brought was the uprising of the Indians. "They are getting bolder in raiding isolated farms. You should instruct your sons what to do if they come here."

Angela looked bewildered. "And what should that be, Harry? I've never even seen an Indian."

"You need a hiding place, not just for your valuables but for yourself and the boys."

"I have no valuables. But I shall give thought to where we could hide – providing, of course, that we have some warning of their approach. Could you send word from the Fort if they are known to be in this area?" She wanted to add that perhaps Archie could come protect them, but the idea quickly passed.

"Yes, Ma'am. I'll come myself." He looked at her with pity.

Harry played tossing a ball with the boys for a few minutes before mounting his horse and disappearing out of sight. Angela sighed, knowing that many weeks lay ahead with only her two sons for companionship.

Wil's naughtiness progressed from doing mischief to brutalizing Kincade. Angela was unaware that she was responsible for much of Wil's combative behavior. Every day she had reason to say, "Wil, can't you behave like Kincade? Can't you do that like your brother? Can't you remember like Kincade? Your brother is so gentle; why are you so cruel-hearted?" Though she didn't mean to, Angela's well-intentioned disciplines fanned a fire of hate burning within Wil's soul.

Since Wil could hardly thrash his mother for the constant comparisons, he chose to attack the object of her praise. If Kincade liked a toy, Wil would break it. If Kincade carried eggs from the hen enclosure, Wil would knock the basket out of his hand. When Kincade could recite the alphabet, Wil tore up the McGuffey Reader. He plotted to trip his brother and make him fall in the mud. When the boys had been put to bed he would push and shove Kincade to the far side until Angela jerked him to the wall and gently laid Kincade in the middle next to her. Wil's hatred of his brother was written all over his face, but Angela was too exhausted from doing chores and maintaining some semblance of peace to even notice his bitter countenance. A five year old boy couldn't possibly have adult emotions – not like the hatred she felt for Archibald Logan.

Angela had explained to her sons that an Indian attack was possible, but not probable since she had nothing of value for them to steal or destroy. Wil immediately strutted around pretending to shoot a wooden gun that his father had given him years before. Kincade climbed onto his mother's lap. "I'll take care of you, Mama. Don't worry." She kissed his head and put him down. Wil ran by them, shooting his gun in their faces. "Bang, bang bang! I killed you, Mama! You're dead!" he yelled.

The day it all happened had dawned clear, warm and without the hint of a breeze. By afternoon Angela had done the wash and was hanging out the garments with Kincade's help. Wil was gathering stones to throw at the goats. Bending down to her basket to pick up the last piece of damp clothing, Angela sensed something was wrong. She looked up. It was as if twelve ghosts had emerged on horseback from the adjoining woods. They slowly approached with absolute silence - no yelps, no war cry, no weapons readied for attack. At first, Angela thought the sun's glare was playing tricks on her. But that changed an instant later when Kincade pointed and asked, "Are those Indians, Mama?"

Angela screamed and dropped the wet garment she held. She moved to clutch Kincade who stood only a few feet away. Instantly, one of the mounted Indians blocked her by moving his big buckskin horse between her and Kincade. The brave used his moccasin to push her back forcefully, but not so hard as to injure her.

Angela regained her balance and moved to grab Wil. But it was too late to help the second boy, for several more horses had formed an impenetrable line with Wil behind them.

"Mama! Mama! Come get me!" The terrified Wil cried out in panic. The Indians continued their silence, moving only as was necessary to separate the two boys from their mother.

The yard carried three sounds: the snorting of the horses as they were jerked this way and that, churning the dry soil, preventing any breach of the line between the mother and her children; Wil's pitiful crying for help; and Angela's fear-stricken screaming as she tried to get past the barricade of riders. "Oh God, help me!" she kept repeating.

She was terrified. She imagined what was sure to happen next. Some of the Indians were certain to rape her. Others would loot and burn the soddy. What few animals she had would be slaughtered, followed by the savages finally butchering her and her two sons.

Angela suddenly became aware that, although Wil's tears fell like rain, Kincade stood dry eyed. Her first-born son looked with fascination at the dark men wearing strange costumes and paint on their faces. Their horses were unlike any that his papa or Harry rode. The animals, too, had paint on their skins and there were neither blankets nor saddles on any of them. "Kincade! Don't look at the savages!" Angela called to him. She could not understand his composure under these terrifying circumstances.

The Indians began to form a circle around the two boys, bunching the children into the center. Angela frantically tried time and time again to break past their blockade. But with each move, the Indians would gently but firmly push or nudge her to stay back. Her knees finally buckled and she fell onto the dirt and sobbed, "What do you want of me? Do your worst, but leave my boys alone."

All the while, the eyes of eleven braves watched the twelfth... a powerful man on the largest black horse. That Indian finally stopped the circling horses by raising his hand to the others. Ignoring Angela, he looked directly at the two boys – first at one and then the other. He was silent for a long moment. Then, for the first time, she heard an Indian speak. Their leader shouted an order in a deep, guttural voice. Angela screamed an echo. With lightning speed he and another brave charged into the center of the circled horses, lifted Kincade and Wil off the ground by the hair, swung them up and over to sit in front of them on their horses.

The entire band of twelve, now fourteen, immediately turned and followed their leader into the woods from where they had first appeared. Not more than ten minutes had passed.

Angela was left unharmed in the dirt-churned yard – more alone than she could have ever imagined.

Her state of shock gave over to bewilderment. All the horrors she had imagined being inflicted by a band of savage Indians didn't happen. What she could never have imagined – and by far the worst – did happen. Her boys had been kidnapped! There was nothing she could do. She must get help, but from whom? As often as she had sworn to cut him out of her life, there was no one but Archie.

Without even going to the house for a shawl she started running across the yard. The main road lay a fair distance from the soddy, but she reached it in less than twenty minutes. Maybe a wagon would come along and she could beg a ride to the Fort which was at least five miles away. Maybe a horseman would swing her up behind his saddle and she could hang on for dear life as he galloped as fast as possible. But the road remained empty.

She ran until her breath gave out and she had to slow down. Her increasing exhaustion forced her to trudge on doggedly, placing one foot in front of the other. She stumbled and fell. She allowed herself to rest for only a moment, keeping her sons' faces in her mind to drive her on once again. She refused to cry for sobs would only sap what strength she had left, but the pain in her heart was akin to tears.

The shadows lengthened and the night insects began to buzz. She had to keep her eyes on the roadway immediately under her feet or she would fear the darkness hiding up ahead. Her legs ached, her feet were numb, and her breath came in short gasps. Her lips were parched and her tongue stuck to the roof of her dry mouth. If the purpose for reaching the Fort was only to save herself, she would have given up hours ago. But the very lives of her boys were dependant on her reaching the army post and the soldiers. Archie would find the boys. He must. She doggedly forced herself to continue.

It was far beyond twilight when she finally saw the wooden gate of the Fort. She fell against it and pushed her hardest, but it was tightly shut for the night. She pounded and yelled, wondering if anyone could hear her weak voice.

She was on her knees, sobbing when she heard a voice from the other side. "Who's there?"

"Thank God," she screamed. "Let me in – let me in. I need help!" The door slowly opened and there stood Harry. His familiar face brought fresh tears to her eyes. "Oh Harry – it's you!" was all she could say.

"Mrs. Logan?" He could hardly believe that the friendly woman he brought supplies to was actually here before him, and apparently in great distress.

"Take me to the Captain, Harry. I have terrible news and desperately need help."

The young man lifted her to her feet. "Yes, Ma'am. The Captain, you say?" He seemed embarrassed.

"Yes, yes. My husband, Archibald Logan, you know that. Hurry! There is no time to waste."

"I'll take you right away, Ma'am." He took her arm for she wavered unsteadily. "The Captain is still in his office."

They walked slowly across the compound and came to the central building. Harry knocked and heard the reply, "Come." They entered a cluttered office lit by a kerosene lamp. An elderly man with white hair, dressed in a Captain's uniform, sat behind a desk reading papers. He looked up. "Yes, what is it?"

Angela stepped forward. "I must speak with my husband, Archibald Logan. It's a matter of life and death."

"I believe Corporal Logan is out on patrol. Mrs. Logan, if you have such an urgent matter perhaps I can help you. I'm Captain David Brooker."

Angela stared at him in disbelief. Corporal Logan? Captain Brooker? Her husband on a patrol instead of in this office? She shook her head, not understanding anything she heard. But there was no time for an explanation.

"Sir, Indians have taken my two boys. They swept into the yard this afternoon and snatched up Wil and Kincade and rode off. There was nothing I could do. God only knows what will happen to them in savage hands. Someone must go after them - immediately." She was breathless and felt so weak that she grabbed for a chair.

"Please be seated, dear lady. Harry, bring her some strong tea. Are you hungry?" She shook her head. "Bring toast anyhow, Harry. And please be quick about it."

Angela liked the fatherly looks of this man. She didn't feel quite so alone any more. She tried to smile, but her lips quivered too much.

"Now tell me exactly what occurred. Take your time. Details

may be important."

Angela relived every sight, every sound, every action. She would not forget a single second of this day for the rest of her life. The Captain sat listening with intent interest and making a few notes as she proceeded with details. The hot tea arrived just as she finished. "Take some refreshment, dear lady. You need it. Shall I add some brandy?" She shook her head. Her hunger was greater than she had realized and she ate the toast with relish. He looked at her with sympathetic eyes.

"Do you mind if I smoke?" He held up a long cigar.

She shook her head. "My papa smoked. The smell of a cigar always reminds me of him." The refreshments made her relax. She felt almost sleepy. They watched one another as the Captain lit the cigar and blew a few smoke rings into the air. His face was solemn.

"I believe I can assure you that your sons will not be tortured or killed." Angela breathed a sigh of relief. "When a tribe has few male children, either because of an epidemic or an abundance of female births, they will steal very young boys and raise them as Indians. I am sure this is why Kincade and Wil were abducted. They are the right age, appear to be in good health, and the fact that you were alone with them - without a man's protection - made grabbing your sons an easy matter. This opinion is coupled with the fact that they caused you no physical harm. They wanted your boys, nothing else. I wouldn't be surprised to learn that these Indians may have been spying on you for some time."

Angela listened to this explanation without much relief. "I must get them back, Captain. You understand how strongly I feel about this. Archibald Logan is my husband. He must find them for me."

He puffed on his cigar. "Of course I understand." He puffed some more. "I can send out Corporal Logan as soon as he returns from his present assignment. You're right. He should be the one to lead a small platoon since he alone can recognize your sons."

The question of searching for her sons having been answered, Angela now became aware that Archie was again being called Corporal. She dared to ask, "Why do you call him Corporal? Archie is a Captain, like yourself."

"No, Madam", he paused. "He was demoted some time ago."

Angela suddenly recalled the last time she'd seen Archie. His uniform had no Captain's insignia. "May I ask why he was demoted?"

Captain Brooker looked at her through the smoke of his cigar. "It is not a pretty picture, Madam. I'm not sure you should want to hear it. You might be quite shocked."

"I have my own picture which is not pretty." Angela modesty opened the tight neck of her blouse, exposing the deep scars carved like the letters 'A' and 'L'. "Nothing you can say about my husband will shock me, Captain." She buttoned the blouse and looked him straight in the eyes. "Tell me."

Captain Brooker ground out his cigar in a dirty ashtray and leaned back in the swivel chair with a sigh. "If you wish. It was before I was assigned to this post so I can only tell you what was told me. God only knows what really happened."

And with that, Brooker began to share Archibald Logan's story with Angela.

CHAPTER 9

This is what only God knew.

*　　*　　*　　*　　*　　*

"DAMN REDSKINS! DAMN squaw whores!" Captain Archibald Logan sat with his two buddies, Lieutenant Kincade and Sergeant Wilson, at a table in a rustic bar in Grey Butte, about seventy-five miles from the Fort where they were stationed. That afternoon their platoon had annihilated an Indian family group traveling between villages with grandparents, a pregnant woman, and several small children. Captain Logan was celebrating. He flicked beer foam from his waxed mustache. "Did you boys know that the only whores in this God forsaken corner of nowhere are Indian squaws? The savages actually sell their wives for a jug of whiskey!" He finished his beer. "And they are filthy. I had to take a bath afterwards."

"Did you pay more than a quarter?" Wilson asked in his usual way, trying to win the favor of Captain Logan.

"For the squaw whore or the bath?" Archie guffawed. "I didn't give her nothing except a good whipping with my crop."

He signaled to the bartender. "This beer is nauseating. Bring me your best whiskey, and if you brewed it yourself I'll run my knife through your fat belly." Logan laughed and stared at the buttons on the cuff of his army uniform with bleary eyes. The whiskey arrived and he sniffed it. "Pew! Nevertheless, to your health, gentlemen, and may it be better than this firewater." He drank it down and belched loudly.

Lieutenant Kincade and Sergeant Wilson lifted their beers. "Here's to you, Captain." They were hoping he wouldn't get so drunk that they would have to tie him on his horse.

"As I was saying, my friends, I dislike with equal vigor the Indians' damn runt papooses. The squaws are prolific, born to breed more Redskin trash to stink up this country." His speech was slurred.

The fifteen new recruits who had initially taken up chairs alongside their Captain cautiously retreated to other sides of the room. Their official orders had been to accompany army supply wagons, which they had done without incident. The Captain's afternoon attack made these young men have doubts about their duty to obey their superior officer. His slaughtering of the Indian family didn't feel right - because it wasn't right. Though some of the soldiers had little love for the Native American, most were good men who understood that they were on lands that had always belonged to the Indians.

But not Captain Logan. He hated Indians. And he would prove just how much with every opportunity that came his way. Maybe when this platoon headed out in the morning he'd again get to teach those savages the superiority of White men.

*   *   *   *   *   *

Takchaweeska, Little White Dove, was crouched, peeking through the tall prairie grasses, her eyes fixed on a herd of antelope she had just spotted. Her brother Tasunke Hinzi, Yellow

Horse, gently increased the tension on the twisted buffalo tendon fastened to each end of the iron wood bow. Little White Dove squealed with delight the instant he released the arrow. The half dozen antelope bolted. Her excitement had alerted them to human presence.

"Oh, they're running away!" The little girl sighed and then fell silent as she saw Yellow Horse frown, lower his bow and turn to his older brother Wapasha, Red Leaf, for censure or approval.

Red Leaf, who had known sixteen winters, smiled broadly at them both. "You must work together," he taught. "One sees the prey, guiding the other for a perfect and quick kill. The second cannot succeed without the first. The first depends on the success of the second. Both reap the reward." Red Leaf came over to them, ruffling Yellow Horse's hair and poking Little White Dove playfully in the ribs.

Yellow Horse knelt to look eye to eye with Little White Dove. "You did well, my sister. Had you not seen the antelope, we would never have come so close. Now, thanks to you, we know their direction and their numbers."

Little White Dove smiled so brightly that the hearts of both boys melted in the warm morning sun. She hugged her brothers as hard as she could. "I will do better next time!"

Little White Dove was Brave Eagle's only daughter, now the sole female in the lodge of the revered Indian Chief. Her mother, Blue Waters, had died bravely giving her birth six winters before. The Chief of the tribe knew that he should take a second wife as custom required. But his soul had not freed itself from his first love, Blue Waters. The time had come when Little White Dove should be taught to cook, to quill moccasins and tan hides for clothes and tepees. More importantly a new mother would tell her the family history, and have her learn the traditional customs and practices of the tribe. Perhaps he should ask Blue Water's sister.

But Brave Eagle always said, "Not today."

From birth Little White Dove had not been strong. When physically taxed, the girl quickly wilted like a parched flower. The tribe's pezuta would listen to her small chest and the rapid beats of her heart which sounded like the pounding hooves of a runaway pony. Her face would flush, and then turn to a grey. But she could be soothed with the sound of the shaking medicine rattle and the strokes of the stiff eagle feather. Color would soon return to her cheeks and the smile on her lips. The Indians considered her frail body proof of her strong spirit, as rare and as special as the first delicate flowers of spring.

Brave Eagle gave wholehearted love to his three children, nurturing them, empowering them, helping them to feel good about themselves, about the joy of learning new things, of respecting the Circle of Life, of the balance between earth, sky, water and fire, forging a deep appreciation in his young offspring for all things good.

The Chief told his two sons to protect Little White Dove, especially when the three ventured away from the village. Red Leaf and Yellow Horse were honored, not only because they were of the same blood, but because of Little White Dove's fragile constitution. She was a gift from the Great Spirit, they were her earthly guardians. With their help, Little White Dove would grow into the woman Brave Eagle knew she could become, a woman so strong in spirit that their entire tribe would prosper from her leadership and wisdom, moon after moon, season after season.

Red Leaf showed every indication that one day he would take his father's place as Chief of their tribe. Yellow Horse, although younger, listened and learned with the same intensity and desire as Red Leaf. Both would grow into the strong and honorable warriors Brave Eagle expected them to become.

"I'm hungry," Little White Dove said, looking up at her older brother.

"I understand, for I, too, am ready to eat." Red Leaf took her hand. "Have you listened and learned from what I have said today?" She nodded.

Yellow Horse stood by, watching his brother's eyes for approval. "I, too, have listened and learned." He greatly admired his sibling, wanting to please him in every way he could. This trip, now two hours from their village, would be filled with even more life lessons. But not ones Red Leaf could ever imagine even in his blackest dreams.

The platoon of new recruits led by Captain Archibald Logan was pinned to the ground beneath the waving prairie grasses not fifty yards from where Red Leaf, Yellow Horse and Little White Dove talked. "Dirty, thieving, Red savages..." hissed Logan under his breath. "Dirty, thieving going-to-be-dead Red savages!"

*   *   *   *   *   *

Brave Eagle shielded his eyes from the bright sun overhead, now beginning its first descent to the western mountains. He had complete trust and faith in his three children. But he was also cautious when it involved their safety and protection. The Chief walked to the tepee of his most honored scout. A baby in a cradleboard stared at him with huge black eyes and then smiled. A naked toddler held up a bow made of a supple twig for him to admire. He patted the heads of the scout's small children. Their mother smiled at Brave Eagle's attention and ceased her quilling of new moccasins.

"Are you well, Ehawee?" he asked Laughing Maiden.

"Oh, yes," she respectfully replied.

"Is your husband here?"

Before she could answer, the hide covering the entrance to the family's tepee opened.   Ozuye Najin, Standing Warrior, stepped out. He stood over six feet tall, fit and muscular as his name implied. A jet black fan of hair crowned his skull, a grizzly bear claw necklace hung at his chest.

"Your children are growing and happy," Brave Eagle said to Standing Warrior.

"I wish them only to be as wise and strong as my Chief."

Brave Eagle smiled. "And with your guidance they shall be."

Standing Warrior waited for Chief Brave Eagle to explain this visit. "I want you to track my three children, out hunting the antelope. They should be south on two horses. Little White Dove rides with Red Leaf, so their tracks will be deeper than those left by Yellow Horse."

The scout nodded.

"Do not let them know of your presense. My sons are proud, and wish me to believe they can fend for themselves and protect their sister. I have confidence in them."

The scout waited.

"But I am also their father and parents have born-in concerns." The Chief smiled at Laughing Maiden. She understood and smiled back.

Standing Warrior nodded and went to retrieve his bow and full quiver from the tepee. He moved quickly to his horse, tied nearby. He easily swung onto the bareback, firmly nudged his feet into the buckskin's sides and galloped from the village.

Brave Eagle looked to the sun, now slightly lower in the sky.

Laughing Maiden could see his brow crease ever so slightly. But it wasn't from the light's glare.

*   *   *   *   *   *

Little White Dove looked like a spirit as she gracefully moved through a field of wildflowers lining the small brook near where the antelope had been. Gurgling water danced over and around smooth stones, catching the bright sunlight and deep blue of the sky in a small pool. The stalks and flower blossoms were so healthy that they kissed the child's waist. She would pick only the prettiest for her father. Brave Eagle was a formidable and towering figure in their tribe, but Little White Dove knew the way to his soft heart. Her bouquet would be her private gift to him for the love she felt. Though they would return with no meat, Little White Dove had never felt happier. Her brothers loved her. Her father adored her. And life, all of life, was sweet and good. She quietly hummed to herself.

Her brothers walked towards the grove of aspen trees where their horses were tied. The magnificent paint horses were two of the tribe's best, chosen by their father for his beloved sons. Yellow Horse and Red Leaf were humble by nature. Neither would flaunt the Chief's preferential treatment of them. Everyone in the tribe showed them fellowship and respect because of the friendliness and regard the sons gave others. Their father had taught them, "You get back what you give out." They knew of no other way. It was the only way.

Captain Logan whispered to Lieutenant Kincade. "Take Sergeant Wilson. Circle around behind the two horses. When the boys come alongside, grab them. Soon as I see you've got them by the throats, I'll snatch the girl."

The Captain turned to look at the fifteen new recruits who waited and watched. He smiled with a twisted grin at the Lieutenant. "Then I'll show these greenhorns a little more fun..."

*   *   *   *   *   *

Standing Warrior knew these lands better than anyone in his tribe. The valleys, the hills, the rivers and plains, all were as familiar as the face of his beautiful wife, Laughing Maiden. The scout's eyesight was perfect, capable of following the tracks of the horses ridden by Red Leaf and Yellow Horse without slowing the breakneck stride of his buckskin horse.

As miles passed, the four hoof prints became fresher. The scout knew he was close when the ground indentations were filled with water leached from the ground. He slowed, finally came to a silent stop, and quietly slipped from the buckskin's back. Brave Eagle did not want his children to be aware of the scout's presence.

Standing Warrior crept forward, careful not to break even the smallest branch. He stopped. The scout sniffed the air. A chill ran down his spine. It was filled with an unmistakable stench of unwashed bodies and whiskey - White men! Mixed with the odor was sound - the terrified scream of a child. It was Little White Dove!

*   *   *   *   *   *

Lieutenant Kincade and Sergeant Wilson obeyed the Captain's orders and shuffled backwards on their bellies, past the green recruits and then dropped into a shallow draw. Keeping low, the two used their considerable military experience to swiftly move toward the Indians' horses. Red Leaf and Yellow Horse casually walked toward their mounts, turning to check on the whereabouts of Little White Dove, who gleefully spun within the rainbow of wild flowers surrounding her. The small creek had a merry voice as it splashed over the rocks and she laughed at its gurgling.

This was a good day.

The ears of the two horses went up, their flanks quivered and nostrils flared. They knew strangers were only yards away, standing silently behind two large aspen trees, concealed by the mature trunks. Red Leaf came up to his pinto, immediately recognizing the horse's nervousness as a sign of danger. He began to warn his brother of something amiss, but it was too late.

The two soldiers sprang from their hiding places and were on the boys within a second, grabbing them from behind, snapping their hands around the boys' throats. Their voices and struggles stopped as all air was choked off by the soldiers' strong grip.

At the same instant, Captain Logan bounded through the creek towards Little White Dove. She was so shocked, she froze, and Logan grabbed her, knocking the breath from her small chest. The girl dropped the bouquet of flowers she had gathered for her father.

The Lieutenant and Sergeant held their grip and dragged the two boys over to Captain Logan, who now stood with Little White Dove pinned to his chest, her feet dangling far from the ground. Her shock was replaced with stark terror.

Yellow Horse shot his right foot forward and then backwards to slam into Wilson's lower leg. The Sergeant howled.

Captain Logan laughed. "Indian runt getting the best of you? What'll your men think, seeing their Sergeant getting beat by a boy?"

Wilson looked back towards the platoon of soldiers standing on the other side of the creek, wide-eyed and slack-jawed at what they were seeing. Then he brought back his free hand, formed a fist, and slammed it into Yellow Horse's ear, nearly knocking the boy unconscious.

"That the best you can do, Sergeant?"

Sergeant Wilson stuttered, "I... uh..."

"Well?!..." said Logan to Wilson.

"Captain, I punched him as hard as I could."

"You're weak, Wilson. I'll take care of him." Without a moment's hesitation, Captain Archibald Logan drew his pistol, cocked the hammer and put a bullet squarely into the stomach of Yellow Horse. The range was so close that the lead tore through the boy's body, flaring the bullet's head into the size of a small mushroom, which exploded out the boy's back, leaving an enormous exit wound, immediately killing the second son of Brave Eagle.

Sergeant Wilson's entire torso was splattered with flesh, bits of bone and blood which sprayed even his face. He was shocked by Captain Logan's murder of the boy, but no more so than the troops standing just twenty feet away.

Little White Dove screamed as her brother crumpled onto the ground, the dirt running red as his body bled out. Red Leaf exploded in rage, smashing the back of his skull into the forehead of Lieutenant Kincade. The crack of bone sounded like a rifle shot. The soldier grunted loudly, releasing his grip on Red Leaf's neck. The boy reared his back into the chest of the Lieutenant. Using the big man's weight as a springboard, he kicked his feet into the face of Captain Logan, not four feet away.

But Logan was fast, even faster than Red Leaf. With a quick cock of his pistol, Captain Logan fired a second round into the forehead of the first son of Brave Eagle.

"Savages!" yelled Captain Logan. "Blood-thirsty savages no better than wild animals!" Little White Dove struggled. There was a pounding in her chest in a way she had never felt before. Something inside her was running faster and harder than the antelope she had spooked not fifteen minutes earlier. Her breath came in ragged pants. A clammy sweat beaded onto her brow, her head began to spin.

Sergeant Wilson and Lieutenant Kincade stood erect, the crumpled bodies of the two Indian boys at their feet, looking into the enraged eyes of Captain Logan. The Captain spun to their troops. "Let this be a lesson to all of you!" he shouted. "Don't ever trust a Redskin. Not unless you want to be torn apart like these two would have done to us if we hadn't surprised them first."

Captain Logan grabbed a fistful of Little White Dove's hair and held her in the air like some piece of meat. "Their females are just as bad, no matter what their size or age. They breed like dogs. I'm going to kill this budding squaw today so that there will be fewer braves I'll have to kill tomorrow!"

The pulsating was running away inside Little White Dove, outracing her ability to live. Her left arm began to ache, her chest felt like a stake had been jammed into it.

"Do you hear me?!" bellowed Captain Logan at the troops, waving his pistol back and forth. "Let this be a warning to all of you! No prisoners, no mercy!" Logan lowered Little White Dove, and yanked her frail body to the creek, stepping into a pool about three feet deep. He held the girl's head by the back of the neck, bringing her face down.

At that moment Little White Dove experienced the strangest and most wonderful sensation of her entire life. All terror left, replaced by a complete and all-consuming calm. It was as though she was completely alone, unafraid and surrounded by a loving and very powerful presense.

She looked into the pool of water and there, looking up at her with the brightest and kindest smile she had ever seen, was the face of the mother who gave her birth - Blue Waters. Little White

Dove could hear her mother speak. "Come, my little one. You have fulfilled your reason for this birth. Your visit here is over. Come be with me now in the Invisible Realm." Little White Dove's fragile heart stopped beating the moment she uttered her last earthly word: "Mother?..."

Captain Logan plunged the small head of Little White Dove below the waters that he intended to make her watery grave. But the girl didn't struggle or resist. For she had already left this world and into the loving aura of the spirit she never knew.

*   *   *   *   *   *

Standing Warrior had peered over the rise that shielded him from the soldiers. He now saw a White man standing in a pool of water. Between his legs, the scout could see the motionless back of Little White Dove submerged beneath the surface. Not ten feet away, the Indian saw the two shattered bodies of Red Leaf and Yellow Horse. Standing Warrior had seen many killing fields, but nothing as brutal as this attack on three innocent children.

He felt himself rising up, quickly reaching for the long knife at his waist, about to charge towards the man now stepping from the pool. He was certain he could kill this man, and just as sure that he, himself, would be murdered by the other soldiers moments later. That did not matter to Standing Warrior. To die for Chief Brave Eagle and his beloved children would be a great honor. But he stopped himself. Letting that man and his soldiers go, to ride and kill another day, would be a disgrace to his people and to his Chief.

Standing Warrior loosened the grip on his knife, memorized the face of that White killer, and crept back to his horse. He leapt silently onto the buckskin's back, being careful as he turned the animal toward the village many miles away. The soldiers must not hear him, or know that the slaughter by one of them had been witnessed.

A fierce wind rose up. A half mile beyond the creek and the bloodied ground, the scout urged his horse to run faster, exerting every muscle and every breath the horse was capable of. The animal was strong, conditioned by long and swift rides chasing buffalo when Standing Warrior hunted. He obeyed every command to outrun the wind, causing an eerie stillness to surround rider and horse as their speed matched the fierce wind blowing behind their backs. The sky suddenly darkened, and a distant clap of thunder boomed across the land, as if the spirits above were furious at the slaughter of children.

"Brave Eagle must know everything that happened. This day must be avenged!"

CHAPTER 10

THE SOLDIERS WERE told to assemble and they rode slowly away from the massacre. It was a strung out platoon, each man deep in his own thoughts, not wanting to have conversation with any who would agree or disagree with the emotions that tore through him. Most were deeply troubled. When they enlisted they had been told that they would probably have to fight Indians. But their experiences on this patrol had not been battles with wild renegades nor war-painted braves attacking helpless ranchers. Captain Logan had first bent his wrath on a family traveling with aged grandparents, an expectant mother, and little children. Then, and perhaps his worst atrocity, was the unprovoked killing of two innocent boys and a beautiful little girl. They were soldiers but they were not butchers.

A few men laughed nervously, hoping to show bravado. They were afraid that their superior officer might see the fright in their eyes. They thought he was a mad man and could just as easily turn on them as he had turned on the Indians if he suspected any insubordination.

Lieutenant Kincade rode well behind Captain Logan. He detested the man, not so much for his brutality, but for his rank. Logan and Kincade had served together in the Civil war, as had Sergeant Wilson. Logan had gained the rank of Captain, not from military knowhow or courageous leadership, but by making sure his Colonel had French brandy and imported cigars which he would steal from the wealthiest plantations they raided. Once he had the commission he strutted like a Napoleon but behaved like a Simon Legree. Lieutenant Kincade was appalled when he learned that Logan had requested him to be his second in command in the western territories. To refuse the appointment would have been throwing his military aspirations to the wind. Captain Logan was a very revengeful superior officer – best to hide his hatred until he could rise above the status of Lieutenant. He secretly hoped that his Captain would someday do something so inexcusable that the bars would be torn off his uniform and the sadistic grin would be wiped off his contemptuous mouth.

Sergeant Wilson was a died-in-the-wool soldier. He had no family, no home, and no special talent that might serve him in another capacity. He followed orders, went where he was sent, and did the jobs assigned him. He didn't think about any alternatives. In fact, he didn't think at all. Others could lead, he would follow. That was the only way he could be sure he was doing the right thing. In the Civil War he had been Logan's drill sergeant and quarter master. The fact that he'd been assigned to go west was an affirmation that he had done well. He would not be condemned nor praised for Captain Logan's behavior.

Riding well ahead of the platoon was Captain Archibald Logan. His head was held high, his posture was rigid, he held his reins with gentlemanly firmness, and his boots were pushed into the stirrups like battering rams. Pride reeked from his countenance. He was too august to allow anyone to ride near him on this day of his triumph.

Day was drawing to a close and everyone was tired. Even the horses were laggard. Heads were nodding and eyes were drooping. Nothing could be seen ahead to warrant readiness and they had already safely traversed the lands to their rear. The recruits wondered if the Captain would bivouac soon or push on to the nearest settlement. Sergeant Wilson decided to ride forward and put the question to their leader. But as he galloped forward he happened to look up.

On a long butte, silhouetted against the flame-red sunset, were forty mounted Indians. For a few moments they held a forbidding pose and then with a resounding battle cry began a lightning fast race down the slope toward the troops. Their piercing shouts and shrill war whoops turned the soldiers' blood into water. As they grew closer their formidable appearance was even more paralyzing. They wore only loincloths, moccasins and necklaces of grizzly bear claws. Their faces, bodies, arms and legs were smeared with paint, and long eagle feathers protruded from the knotted coils of their jet black hair, while others had shaved heads except for a thick, finger-wide band from forehead to nape of the neck. A full quiver dangled from their backs. Each arrow identified its owner by the arrangement of colored feathers, for a man could only scalp those whom he had personally killed. A scalping knife was fastened to their thighs. The braves split into two groups, going right and left, quickly forming a circle around the panicky soldiers. The dust kicked up was blinding and choking. The barbaric howls of the Indians and the outcries of the soldiers were deafening.

The hides of the Indians' snorting horses were also painted and many scalps hung from their manes and tails. The braves rode without reins, using both hands for their bows and arrows. These were buffalo runner horses and needed only the pressure of their rider's legs to direct them in any maneuver or direction. Many of the soldiers had not even loaded their guns that day and those who had could not aim at the zigzagging horses. The Indians let fly their arrows with deadly accuracy. Men fell from their horses with blood spouting from open wounds. Once an enemy was on the ground, his killer flipped the man face down. With his foot on the shoulder of the victim, the Indian withdrew his knife and cut a triangle from the top of the forehead to the base of the neck. He then gave one mighty pull and ripped the hair and scalp from the still alive victim. With a bone chilling death cry, he would hang the scalp from the cord of his loincloth and ride on to kill again.

Lieutenant Kincade tried to see through the mayhem. "Captain! Captain Logan!" he shouted at the top of his lungs. "Tell them to cluster in the center and place their horses for a barrier." There was no response. "Captain! For God sake, tell these men to fire ahead of their running horses!" Those were his last words as an arrow pierced his throat and he fell under the hooves of his horse.

Sergeant Wilson had never been a leader of men. He hadn't even participated in a Civil War battle, always staying behind to send supplies up front. "Captain!" His voice was trembling with panic. "Tell me what to do! What should we all be doing? Captain!" He spun his horse in circles, hoping he would see his commanding officer through the turmoil. He was suddenly aware that he was falling. He clutched his stomach and his hand felt an arrow deeply imbedded in the roll of fat. "I'm going to die," he whispered. "Captain Logan, help me. I'm going to die." Bubbles of blood filled his mouth and his eyes closed before his scalp was taken.

Sixteen corpses lay in grotesque positions as they had died, some falling from their horses, others running from an attacker. Their mutilated heads rested in bloody pools. Lieutenant Kincade knew he had been mortally wounded by the arrow, but he had dragged his crushed legs to a place of concealment in the rocks at the base of the long butte. He waited for the Indian who had shot the arrow lodged in his neck to return to scalp him. The wait was not long. The brave stood over him, looking at the shaft with his personal feathers on it – proof of his deed. He yanked it out and Lieutenant Kincade screamed with pain. He would now bleed to death. The Indian smiled, touched him on the chest, and strode away.

The horde of triumphant Indians rounded up the captured horses and started back to their village. They stripped off their loincloths and swung their display of scalps around their heads, singing a victory chant. Only two remained on the field of battle. They walked from body to body, turning over those whose faces could not be seen.

"Is he one of these?" Brave Eagle asked Standing Warrior. The scout shook his head. "Will you remember his face if ever you see it again?"

"Until my dying day."

* * * * * *

When Brave Eagle returned to the village he found that the bodies of Red Leaf, Yellow Horse, and Little White Dove had already been wrapped in ceremonial red robes and placed up on a funeral platform. In respect for their Chief, the tribe stayed in their lodges, understanding that their presence would only accentuate their leader's grief.

Brave Eagle fell to his knees as he ached for his murdered children. As day fell into night, he cried aloud, "I know that all which is mysterious, powerful and sacred is Wakan Tanka – The Undiscovered Law. It has always been and always will be. But how can I accept its wisdom when my children are its victims?" Hours passed.

Under the light of a full moon, a vision appeared. They were Iatiku and Nautsiti, the two sisters who had created all of mankind. The spirit apparitions were not alone. There, in the ghostly moonlight, wafted the Wakanpi, invisible beings who exercised power and control over everything.

Brave Eagle had been taught by his grandfathers, and they had been taught by ancestors before them, that it was essential for humans to please these spirits. He whispered to the vaporous vision, "I know that the great knowledge and wishes of the Wakanpi are incomprehensible to ordinary flesh and blood. But I, Brave Eagle, must understand your needs, and what I am to do regarding the deaths of my children."

Brave Eagle released all his human constraints and waited. Then, he heard voices that made no sound. "You must turn to your tribe's Shaman, Man Of The Mysterious Voice, whose special knowledge comes from his dreams with the Spirit Ones. The Shaman will act as a medium through which the power of the Wakan Tanka, Iatiku and Nautsiti, and the Wakanpi will flow. These Spirits bid you, Brave Eagle, to seek counsel with Howahkan, Man Of The Mysterious Voice, the holiest of your people."

The Chief bowed his head as the apparitions stared through his eyes and into his soul, disappearing in the assurance their will would be done.

The morning following Brave Eagle's vision, the Chief sat before Man Of The Mysterious Voice in his lodge. Fragrant smoke drifted up from the center fire pit. The Shaman passed the pipe. The Chief accepted, acknowledging respect by puffing quietly. Both knew why they were together, and what must be done.

For several minutes they remained thus and then, placing the pipe at the edge of the fire, Man Of The Mysterious Voice took his medicine bag from its resting place over his heart. Opening the leather pouch with his withered hands, he withdrew a carved stone of gypsum. The fetish had eyes of turquoise set with pitch from the juniper tree. Brave Eagle recognized it as one of the four prey animals: the Cougar.

Man Of The Mysterious Voice spoke as the ritual began. "Your children's deaths are not reconciled by The Keeper of the Soul." The smoke from the lodge fire floated around the Holy Man who stared deeply into Brave Eagle's eyes. "It is you who must resolve things left undone, healing your Spirit, and restoring peace to the greater community. Only then will your deceased children transcend into the Spirit World."

Man Of The Mysterious Voice held the fetish in the palms of his hands, his hushed prayers joining the spirits and the powers of the other prey animals - the Grizzly, the Wolf, and the Lynx - to the spirit of their brother, the Cougar. As Brave Eagle watched, the Shaman began to sway his clasped hands to the four directions. His voice began a chant:

"It comes alive
It comes alive, alive, alive.
In the east mountain
The Cougar comes alive
In the east mountain, comes alive.
Through this prey animal
You will be reconciled."

The Shaman fell silent. Man Of The Mysterious Voice placed the Cougar fetish into the hands of Chief Brave Eagle. And the two waited. Not a word spoken, not a muscle moved as the two waited for the sun to cross the sky, retreat to the far side and sink behind the mountain. Not a word as darkness descended on the Indian village.

During this time, the Cougar became alive.

Man Of The Mysterious voice spoke. "Drink the blood of the Cougar..."

Brave Eagle felt mysteriously imbued with the knowledge and power to one day destroy the White man who had committed the murders of Takchaweeska, Tasunke Hinzi and Wapasha.

CHAPTER 11

LIEUTENANT KINCADE HAD lain in his rock hideout listening to the fast fading war whoops. He lifted his head high enough to see two powerful Indians remaining. They inspected each fallen soldier as if looking for someone. When they rode away he fell back to die. But another sound made him look again. The Indians were not the only ones to ride away from the scene of battle. A lone horseman emerged from the rocks not far from the Lieutenant's concealment and galloped away as fast as the horse could race.

When the Indians first appeared, Captain Archibald Logan had been riding ahead of the platoon. As the warriors descended on the soldiers, Logan panicked. His bravado with green recruits and children evaporated into what he truly was: a complete and utter coward. Instead of being trapped within the Indians' circle, he galloped away and hid, leaving his troops to fend for themselves, escaping in the dust of pounding hooves and confusion of war cries. Lieutenant Kincade watched his commanding officer leave the scene of carnage, and he swore he would live to tell of this spineless desertion by the most despicable man he had ever known.

*   *   *   *   *   *

For two days Logan galloped his horse to its endurance, stopping only for rest when he thought it would die beneath him. The beast meant nothing to him. He must return to the Fort and report an Indian attack on his valiant troops. When he knew he was only an hour away, he stopped to make himself less presentable. He killed a rabbit and splashed the blood over his spotless uniform. He ripped a sleeve as though an arrow had torn through it. He smeared his face with sweat from the horse and brushed sand in his hair and mustache as if he had fallen. He knew he looked the part of a battle-scarred soldier and he was pleased with his efforts. No one would suspect he had not been in the worst of the fight. As a final touch he cut a deep gash in his horse's flank.

When Captain Archibald Logan galloped through the gates he rode straight to the dispensary and slid from his horse, feigning to fall from exhaustion. He stumbled up the steps and burst open the doctor's door.

"Doctor Burrows, thank God you're here!" he gasped. "My men!... my troops... ambushed by Indians! After killing six of those savages, I barely escaped with my life! Quick! We've got to get back to save any who may still be alive. There's no time to waste!" He convincingly collapsed in a chair.

The old doctor was shocked, looking at the blood covering the soldier. "Captain, you've obviously just come through hell. I'll order two buckboards and leave immediately." Logan got unsteadily to his feet as if to join the doctor. "No, no, Captain. You're in no condition to move. You must stay here."

"But Doctor..." said Logan in a shaky voice. "My men! They need me by their sides if they are wounded or dying."

The doctor knew he was in the presence of a true hero. "Where did this take place?"

"By the long butte straight to the west. I have ridden hard, but I'll lead you there..."

"I insist, you're in no condition!" the doctor said as he turned from Logan to look at his battered horse just outside the door opening. "Your horse is wounded. It will die without care. Please," pleaded the doctor. "Let me examine your wound before I go." The doctor started to remove Logan's blouse, but the Captain stopped him.

"No, Doctor. There are men out there whose lives may be saved if you hurry." Logan pretended resignation, holding his hand over an imaginary wound. "I'll tend to myself – you go to them. God bless you – but don't delay an hour!"

The doctor gathered medical supplies from his office and summoned soldiers to prepare two rigs for emergency conditions and immediate departure. When Logan saw them pass through the gate he went to his own quarters, took a hot bath, put on a clean uniform, and lit a cigar. The only soldiers the doctor would find would be dead, but as their Commanding Officer he would give them a proper funeral when their bodies were brought back.

*   *   *   *   *   *

The trip was long, but Doctor Burrows had no trouble locating the area of the massacre for vultures circled overhead. As they drew nearer, coyotes were snarling over the corpses. He had seen much death in the Civil War but he was sickened at the sight. Some of the soldiers who accompanied him retched in the tall grass without shame.

"There is nothing I can do here," the doctor said. "Please wrap the bodies as best you can and load up the wagons. We'll not stay longer than the time it takes you." He turned away and walked toward the rocks, attempting to calm himself by rolling tobacco into a smoke.

To his amazement he heard a weak voice calling him. "Doc, it's Lieutenant Kincade. I'm here... alive. Can you hear me? Help me. I'm over here."

The doctor dropped his smoke and rushed to the rocks near by. He was shocked at the condition of the officer but ecstatic that at least one had survived. "Thank God! Let me look at your wounds."

"No need, Doc. I've been praying someone would find me – not so I could live but that I could tell what happened here."

"Save your telling until I give you some morphine to ease your pain." The doctor turned to fetch the narcotic. "Your brave Captain Logan already told me what happened."

Lieutenant Kincade grimaced, imagining the lies Logan must have used. "No need. I've only got a few breaths left and I won't waste them on thanking you for your help. Just listen."

*   *   *   *   *   *

Angela sat in stunned silence during Captain Brooker's narration. She had tears running down her cheeks but no sobs escaped her lips.

The Captain ground out his cigar in the dirty ashtray and looked at Angela with sad eyes. "And that, my dear lady, is the story of why your husband was demoted to Corporal. Not only were his actions excessively brutal with the Indians with whom we have been trying to negotiate a peaceful co-existence, but the cowardly desertion of his men was reprehensible."

"Why wasn't he given a dishonorable discharge?"

"I wondered that myself. But as I said, I was brought here to replace him and wasn't present at the time of the trial. My understanding is that your husband claimed Lieutenant Kincade made up the whole story because he was insanely jealous of his superior officer. That he had never done any of the things the Lieutenant claimed."

"What was Doctor Burrow's response to that?"

"Only that the statement of a dying man should be honored. He believed every word Kincade told him. But since there were no other witnesses, your husband was demoted and given a prison sentence." He cleared his throat. "I have not been honest with you, dear lady. Corporal Logan is not on patrol. He is still incarcerated, serving out his sentence. But he will be returning to duty before long."

"And you will send him to find my sons?"

"Yes, I will. However returning him to Indian Territory is not necessarily wise. If there were anyone else who could recognize the boys I would prefer to assign them."

"Your man Harry knows my Kincade and Wil."

The Captain smiled ever so slightly. "I would sooner send a lamb into a lion's den than send Harry to the Indians. No, we will wait for Corporal Logan. Perhaps he will vindicate himself for his transgressions."

She nodded, but without much conviction. "Thank you, Captain, for telling me the truth."

"I'm sorry it was so painful to hear."

"Archie can give me no more pain, except failing to find my boys. I must go home now."

"It's very late, Mrs. Logan. You really must stay with Mrs. Brooker and me tonight."

"But I have animals that need tending and the cabin is wide open, I left in such a hurry."

"Nothing that can't wait until tomorrow. I have some work to finish here but Harry can take you to meet my wife. You'll like her. She's motherly." He smiled. "She'll want you to call her Harriet."

"You're being very kind."

"I'll have Harry take you home in our buggy after breakfast. I understand he brings you supplies. I will get a report from him each time and he will relay messages back and forth between us. And, Mrs. Logan, if there's anything else I can do please don't hesitate."

She stood and her tears fell again. "My boys – just find and return my boys to me..."

PART TWO

CHAPTER 12

I N THE FIVE years since his birth, Kincade had never felt afraid. He simply did not know what the word
meant. His mother used the "afraid" word. "I'm afraid
you'll fall. I'm afraid you'll get lost. I'm afraid Indians will come."
He understood if she was sad or angry. He had felt sadness and
anger himself. But "fear", no.

Now, as he clung to the mane of the Indian's horse, he wondered
why he had a tightening in his stomach. Was this what she meant
when she said "afraid"? Was he afraid he would fall off the horse?
Was he afraid he'd never see his mother again? He wished the
"afraidness" in his stomach would go away. It finally began to sub-
side when he could no longer hear his mother's screams, perhaps
because there was so much strangeness to take its place.

Kincade had never been on a horse. He had stood beside his
father's or Harry's mounts, but he hadn't dared to even touch them.
They were so large, their muscles rippled with power. Now he was
high above the ground astride the biggest, blackest animal he had
ever seen. As the Indian held him tight, Kincade pretended he was
part of the horse – like its mane, or big ears, or long tail. When it
galloped fast it was like the wind blowing, when it walked slowly it
was like rain falling. Kincade pretended he, himself, had become
wind and rain.

There was much newness to see. Mother had never let him or Wil go into the woods where she gathered fuel for the stove. "I'm afraid you'll wander off," she had said. Now he was deep in the forest with trees so tall that at times he couldn't see the sky. Sunlight danced through the branches in flickering patterns. There was a smell that was not like the apple tree next to the soddy.

The horse splashed through a stream. The only water Kincade had ever seen came from the well and filled a bucket or the trough. Now water was in a long, wide ribbon and made wonderful noises and threw little rainbows under the horse's hooves. Sometimes it sprayed his face and he laughed. He tried to turn around to tell the Indian this was fun, but the man's face showed no emotion and his stern mouth didn't welcome talking.

They passed out of the trees and began traveling into brush-covered hills. The way went uphill, and then downhill, and then back up again. Kincade had thought all land was flat like the yard outside the soddy. He had thrown little pebbles, but here there were rocks as big as his home. The Indian who had grabbed him rode ahead of all the others. Kincade wondered how far back Wil was.

The shadows deepened and darkness approached. Kincade began to grow terribly sleepy. The Indian had to straighten him up several times when he dozed. Finally the band stopped. Kincade's eyes were heavy, and as he was pulled from the horse he fell into someone's arms. He was led into some bushes to relieve himself. Then he was laid on a soft furry rug inside a dark place. A long cord was fastened to his wrist and the Indian brave demonstrated that the other end would be fastened to his own wrist, in case Kincade thought of running away. He had no such thought. He only wanted to go to sleep, which he did immediately.

Kincade awakened by a gentle touch behind his ear. Without being startled, he slowly opened his eyes and looked at a man with the oldest face he had ever imagined. Deeply set wrinkles were imbedded from brow to neck, and the eyes were half covered with drooping lids. The big, hooked nose looked like crumpled paper. The parched skin of his entire half-covered body sagged. The man smiled with a mouth that had very few teeth. He spoke strange, soft words that Kincade could not understand, so he just answered, "I'm Kincade." He pointed to his chest. "Kincade." The old Indian held out his boney hand for the boy to sit up and spoke to him again. "I'm Kincade," the boy repeated as he looked around. Where was he? He didn't know a hiding place could be made of leather. It was quite dark inside but faint light came in through an open flap. The old Indian led him outside.

Dawn had long since past. Kincade rubbed his eyes to get used to the bright sunlight. He looked and saw more people than he had ever imagined. He tried to count them on his fingers and bare toes, but there were too many. He never imagined there could be so many people. Everyone was doing a job – busy, but not hurrying. The encampment was quiet for so much activity. The children seemed to be playing happily but not noisily. Indian women with long, black braids, wearing knee-length, leather dresses were hauling and packing and loading leather bags and rolls onto poles. The longer ones were fastened to the sides of horses, the shorter to the sides of dogs. Kincade had never seen a dog but there were drawings of them in the coloring book. These dogs were much larger, with long legs and they looked very strong.

The old Indian took Kincade's hand and led him to a place where he demonstrated that he could relieve himself. When they returned none of the leather sleeping places were in sight. A woman gave him a piece of strange tasting meat and a drink of water. She said something, and her voice was soft and kind. "I'm Kincade," he told her. "Kincade." Not knowing what else to do, he sat cross legged where the sleeping place had been and looked around, waiting.

Finally the Indian brave with whom he had ridden the previous day came and lifted him again onto the big, black horse, easily swinging up behind him.   It was from this height that Kincade first saw Wil. His brother was on the back of one of the big dogs. Kincade waved and shouted to him. "Wil! Look at me! I'm riding a horse!"

Wil's face contorted with envy. He started to yell something in return, but an older boy took the dog by the scuff of the neck and led it further back in the line. "Bye, Wil," Kincade waved again and gave no further thought to his brother as the Indian brave took his place with those heading the wide column.

In the lead were fifteen mature men on handsome horses. All had feathers in their thick black hair. They wore leather leggings but were bare-chested. Most wore necklaces of big animal claws. These were followed by young braves on frisky animals. They rode proudly with bravado banter among them. The women were next, walking with babies strapped in cradleboards on their backs and youngsters beside them trying to keep up. Toddlers as well as children about Kincade's age rode dogs just like Wil. Last came the pack horses and pack dogs, dragging the worldly goods of the tribe. A few old men and old women, too sick to ride or walk, were also carried on the drags. The procession was strung out over several miles and moved slowly except for scouts who galloped in advance and then returned to report on the way ahead to the principal leaders. Stops were made for food and water, but these were infrequent and brief.

Kincade's eyes and ears were constantly alert for animals and birds, both familiar and strange.   He recognized deer with big antlers from the coloring book Auntie Agnes had sent him. Jack rabbits had ears twice as long as the cotton tails that raided his mama's vegetable garden. For the first time he saw antelope that stood like deer but had different markings and the horns didn't have branches. He saw a pack of coyotes slink out of sight and later heard their howling. Prairie dogs popped out of their holes and barked as the Indians passed. There were snakes and lizards and toads among the rocks, fish and frogs in the streams. Big, noisy birds sailed overhead on wide-spread wings. Other strange birds hopped or ran along the ground on all sides of them. Some sat in the trees, singing or squawking. So much excitement for a little boy! Kincade tried to remember everything he saw and heard.

When the leaders in front signaled that they would go no further, the people and horses and dogs formed a large circle. Some of the women began to assemble small overnight shelters with short poles and six skin-covers. Others began fires by twirling sticks into wood shavings. The men took their horses to a nearby stream. Children who were not too tired chased one another and played with simple toys. Kincade was as fascinated with the camp activity as he had been with the changing scenery and wild life. He thought about his mother, but no tears came to his eyes. He thought about Wil, but made no effort to find him. The only person he looked for was the old Indian who soon brought him a wooden bowl filled with hot soup. There was soft meat and knotty roots floating in fatty juice but there was no spoon or fork to eat with. Kincade watched as the old Indian used his fingers for his own bites and then tipped the bowl to drink the liquid. The boy did the same.

For three days the routine for rising and traveling, stopping and eating, quitting and sleeping was always the same. Then on the fourth day, excitement ran through the weary travelers as they came to a rise. There in the valley below were many, many tents, larger than the six-skin tent he had slept in on previous nights. There was much talking among the women and the excited children were allowed to run ahead. The Indian on the horse with Kincade pressed his knees against his mount and it went at a faster pace – not a gallop, but a quick, dignified walk. Others in the lead party had done the same and they all pulled on the jaw-thongs until the horses were in a straight line. Scouts waved robes from the knoll signaling that relatives approached. Before the entire assembly began the descent toward the encampment, the old Indian rode up to the side of the big, black horse and with strong arms lifted the boy onto his own mount. The Indian brave rode toward the village just as the other leaders did - without any child riding with him.

Kincade now rode with the old Indian. He watched as many people came running toward them, the women emitting trilling sounds and the men calling in shouts and joyful whoops. He looked at the many dwellings. He wondered if he was going to stay here forever, and if so, what was Mama going to do without him? Tears filled his eyes as he remembered The Happy Song. They rolled down his cheeks and the old Indian held him closer as they followed the horsemen into the village.

CHAPTER 13

NGELA GOT OUT of the buggy and thanked Harry for bringing her home. She sat down on the porch chair and stared around at the silent and empty yard where her sons had once played. Her lips slowly formed The Happy Song. In a whisper, she sang, "Mother doesn't have any little boys; poor lonesome Mother. Mother says to God; please send back my little boys; or else take me to You in heaven." It was not a happy song any more.

She had no energy for the things she knew must be done. The washing she had been hanging out when the Indians kidnapped her children lay untouched. The goats had not been milked for two days. The chickens not fed. Dirty dishes were still on the table, crusty pans on the cold stove, the children's toys scattered here and there. Angela just sat in a daze whispering The Unhappy Song over and over.

Twilight found her in the same chair. Darkness poured over her like suffocation. When the full moon rose she didn't see the soft light flooding the yard. When the sun crept over the horizon she hardly noticed the brightness. Stunned, she was as much alone now as she would be in a grave.

The need to go to the outhouse finally roused her. She stood and her legs almost gave way, but she grabbed the back of the chair and steadied herself. With all her might, she tried to steel herself. "I must be ready when my boys are brought home," she thought. "I will have fresh bread for them and apple sauce and maybe I'll even kill a chicken for a good stew." She stumbled off the porch, into the yard. "They haven't been gone long. Surely Archie will find them." She moved like a robot, not believing a word that she said to herself. She began sobbing anew. "What if I never see Kincade again!" She caught herself and added, "Wil, too, of course."

*   *   *   *   *   *

The new arrivals chose to set up their village in a circle by a tributary of the main stream. There was a sheltering butte and thick woods. The women quickly went to work unloading the drags and arranging long poles and skins for eighteen dwellings. The old Indian lowered Kincade to the ground. The boy looked for the big Indian who had kidnapped him, but only a woman with thick, black braids worked nearby. The old Indian spoke to summon her. Responding, she took the boy by the hand and led him to a spot where he would be out of the way.

She pointed to herself and said, "Kimimela Weeko," which meant Pretty Butterfly. Then she pointed to Kincade with a questioning look on her face. He hesitated for only a moment and then smiled and pointed to himself. "Kincade. Kincade." She repeated slowly as if the sound was difficult for her to pronounce. "Kincade." He smiled and nodded rapidly. They both laughed and Kincade sat down cross-legged on the soft grass and watched. Once again his fascination kept him from being afraid or lonely. It never occurred to him to look for Wil.

Pretty Butterfly lashed three sturdy poles together at one end with a long rope and then motioned to Kincade to help her raise them. He jumped up and hoisted with all his strength. She spread the unfastened ends apart to form a tripod. More than a dozen other smooth poles were leaned against the three and she spaced their ends evenly in a circle. To secure the top, she walked the long rope around and around three times and then she and Kincade pulled all the poles tightly together.

She next dragged a large folded cover to an open area and carefully spread it out. Many tough buffalo hides had been sewn together to form a semi-circle large enough to cover the framework. There were softer flaps like two big slices of pie sewn near a cutout half-moon in the center. "What are they for?" Kincade wondered but didn't ask. There were painted figures and symbols in red, yellow, white, and black decorating the cover. "Kind of like my coloring book," he thought.

Pretty Butterfly sprinkled water lightly over the cover so it would be more flexible before she tied it onto a raising pole. Another woman left her work to help hoist the heavy hides and wrap the cover around the scaffolding. Once it was in place, the woman called to a boy about Kincade's size to close the overlapping sides. He began five feet up from the bottom, securing the two sides together with long, pointed pins made of hard wood. He inserted them through precut slots in the tough hide. He pushed them until they stuck out both sides of the slots. The light-weight boy climbed them like a ladder in order to reach higher. He stepped gingerly, going up and up, inserting more pins to join the two sides as he went. He stopped just below where the poles stuck out of the half-moon cutout. The funny flaps hung free. Having done his job, the boy descended down the wooden pins with lively steps, and he and his mother left. Kincade had been fascinated. "That looked like fun. Maybe I can do that some time."

The place where the two sides came together at the bottom had not been fastened. Pretty Butterfly tied a piece of skin over this entrance. She finished the exterior by going around the edge and pegging the hides to the ground through slits in the cover. As she walked, she placed a rock at the base of each pole, helping to hold it secure.

Kincade watched and learned without talking. Now Pretty Butterfly came to stand by his side. She pointed to the structure and said, "Tepee." Kincade nodded his understanding. They had just made a tepee. "Tepee," he repeated.

Pretty Butterfly began carrying bundles inside. She motioned to Kincade to help and he followed her with smaller bundles that weren't too heavy. Then he sat cross-legged on the floor and watched.

She began by tying a soft skin lining to the poles all around the interior. It rested on the floor, covering the open space under the outer cover. Then she scooped out a shallow hole directly in the center. She lined it with stones and scattered dry twigs and fragrant leaves over the surface. She left the tepee to get a small flame from the buffalo horn which had been ceremonially carried from the last camp. Carefully placing this in the pit, she fanned the embers until a flame burst and soon the interior began to smell of sage.

Pretty Butterfly took Kincade's hand and led him outside. She pointed for him to look up to the top. She then lifted two light-weight poles so that the ends fit into pockets in the two funny flaps. By moving the poles she could open or close the hole at the top. Kincade clapped his hands. Rain couldn't get in but smoke could get out. This was better than the chimney at Mama's soddy which failed at both efforts.

The two carried more of Pretty Butterfly's bundles into the tepee and she began unpacking household items and putting them around the walls. She went back and forth for everything seemed to have a proper place. Kincade grew weary of watching her arrange containers and paunches, large and small bags, clothing and sleeping robes, and a man's weapons. So he went outside again and sat cross-legged in front of the tepee to see what else was going on.

That was when he first saw Wil. His brother was throwing rocks at the pack animals, making them skittish and difficult to unload.

One woman had placed her folded tepee cover on the ground and Wil climbed on top of it and jumped up and down. She grabbed him by the straps of his overalls and dragged him to where Kincade sat. She plopped him beside his brother and scolded him with words he couldn't understand – and Kincade guessed they were what Mama often said. When she marched back to her work, Wil stuck his tongue out at her.

Wil glared at Kincade, then he starting singing a little song. "Kincade is oh so goodie-good, and Wil is oh so badie-bad. But Wil likes to be badie-bad, and he hates goodie-goodie Kincade." And with that, he gave his brother a strong push which toppled Kincade over backwards. He was about to lunge on top of him with his fists clenched when the big Indian who had kidnapped Kincade came toward the tepee leading the big, black horse. He had evidently taken it to the river for its coat glistened with fresh water. The big Indian jerked Wil to his feet. His eyes were blazing, but he didn't strike the boy. Instead he marched him - feet barely touching the ground - back to the working women. They didn't look too happy to have the trouble-maker in their presence, but none spoke a word.

Kincade sat up and folded his legs again. He said nothing when the big Indian pulled him to his feet and looked at him with hard eyes. He pointed to his chest and said in a deep, gruff voice, "Mahpee Paytah." Then he pointed to Kincade's chest. "Cicila."

The boy blinked for a moment trying to understand. Then he remembered how he and the woman had exchanged names. He pointed to his chest. "Kincade."

The big Indian folded his arms and repeated in an even deeper, firm voice. "Cicila!"

Kincade mimicked his determined voice and also folded his

arms. "Kincade!"

"Cicila! Cicila! Cicila!"

Kincade stomped his foot. "Kincade! Kincade! Kincade!"

The man looked over at Pretty Butterfly. She shyly whispered, "Kincade."

He turned back to the boy. Pointing to himself, he once again said, "Mahpee Paytah." Then he pointed to the boy and said, not quite so firmly, "Kincade." The boy grinned and nodded without showing any triumph.

The man walked around for a few minutes. Then he returned. He held out one hand and said, "Mahpee Paytah." He held out the other hand and said, "Kincade." Then he clasped both hands together in a firm grip. "Mahpee Paytah-Kincade."

Kincade knew what this gesture meant. He now belonged to an Indian man named Sky Fire and an Indian woman named Pretty Butterfly. What he really wanted to know was, would he ever see the old Indian again?

CHAPTER 14

KINCADE WAS AWAKENED with a gentle touch behind his ear. He opened his eyes slowly and saw the wrinkled face of the old Indian. He looked for Pretty Butterfly who had slept on a robe to the left of the entrance and for Sky Fire whose robe was at the back of the tepee. His own robe was between them but not close to either. Both Pretty Butterfly and Sky Fire were gone.

The old Indian smiled reassuringly. He pointed to the boy's chest. "Kincade." Then he pointed to himself. "Kangee Kohana." In this way he said his name was Swift Raven. But Kincade shook his head and pointed to him. "Old Indian."

The ancient one looked bewildered. So Kincade pointed to both of them again and repeated. "I'm Kincade. You're Old Indian."

"Odian?" The words were run together and Kincade shook his head.

Very carefully he said, "OLD – INDIAN!"

This time the wrinkles crinkled with understanding and pleasure. He pointed to himself. "OLD INDIAN." He liked the name. He reached for the boy's hand and they went outside.

Swift Raven picked up a bundle beside the tepee and they went toward the main stream where Kincade heard splashing and laughter. Naked boys, his age and older, were romping and dunking one another beneath knee-deep, rapidly flowing water. They stopped when Kincade approached, but after a few words from Swift Raven they went back to their aquatic playing.

Kincade didn't know what to do. The deepest water he had ever been in was his weekly bath in Mama's big wash tub. Mama had never let him and Wil go naked, let alone play naked. He showed his bewilderment. "Old Indian, am I supposed to do what those boys are doing?"

Swift Raven, sensing his dilemma, led him away from the boisterous youngsters to a quiet channel of gently flowing water. He scooped stones to form a dam and soon there was a large but shallow pool with a sandy bottom. Then Swift Raven pulled off his leather leggings and stood naked except for a loincloth. He motioned for Kincade to do the same.

The two stood ankle deep in the cold water until Kincade's feet stopped tingling. Then Swift Raven began splashing the water onto the boy's calves, knees, and thighs. Just for fun, Kincade splashed him back. "I'll show you, Old Indian!" The dam held and the water deepened. Soon the two were as playful and wet as the boys in the main stream and Kincade's body had been thoroughly washed. As a final coup d'état Swift Raven pushed Kincade's head under the water and held him there for a few seconds. The boy emerged unafraid and laughing. "I can do that too, Old Indian." He tried to jump on Swift Raven's back to bring him down for a similar dunking. The old Indian smiled. Kincade would not be afraid to play with the other boys when they came to bathe in the water tomorrow.

Thoroughly exhausted and hungry, Kincade took his coveralls from the bush where they had been hung and dried himself. But when he started to put them on Swift Raven took them from his hands and tossed them aside. He unrolled the package that he had brought and held up leggings like his own but Kincade's size. There was also a small leather shirt with fringe up the sleeves and a pair of moccasins.

Kincade couldn't believe it! The only clothes he had ever gotten were from Auntie Agnes and they were well-worn hand-me-downs. These were new! Swift Raven gestured that he should put them on, and they all fit perfectly! The moccasins felt strange on his feet which had become calloused from going barefoot all summer. But they were soft and pretty, embroidered with colored designs.

His Mama had taught him to always say thank you. So he did. "Thank you, Old Indian." The words were not understood but the look on Kincade's face said everything.

They went back to the circle of tepees and Swift Raven left Kincade to find his place alone. All the women had been cooking over big fires since dawn. They had heated fist-size rocks in the flames until they were red hot. Then they dropped them in leather paunches filled with water. When bubbles signaled it was time for cooking they had added bits of meat, berries, roots and herbs. Now the soup was ready. The smell made Kincade's mouth water. Pretty Butterfly saw Kincade and motioned for him to sit next to Sky Fire. The big Indian looked at the new clothes and grunted. Kincade wasn't sure if it was with approval or just surprise.

Pretty Butterfly filled Sky Fire's wooden bowl first and then Kincade's. She sat by the fire to add more hot stones to the soup. The big Indian signaled for several refills and she was immediately there to ladle out the most succulent pieces. Kincade was satisfied with just one bowl-full. He sat watching, not knowing if he could leave. Finally Sky Fire turned his bowl upside down and stood to go, so Kincade turned over his bowl as well. Not until both had left the eating circle did Pretty Butterfly ladle a bowl for herself. What was left was mostly broth.

Finished, she began wiping out the bowls with big leaves. Kincade was quick to help her, just as his mama had taught him to wash dishes. He carried them into the tepee. He watched Pretty Butterfly roll up her sleeping robe so he rolled up his and placed it against the liner. He looked around for anything else he could do, but she waved him outside with a smile.

Kincade sat cross legged in front of the tepee and looked around. Nearby young boys were spinning cones made of wood, betting on whose would stay upright the longest. Seeing Kincade, they stopped and looked at him with curious eyes. He said, "I'm Kincade." But at his words they ran away laughing.

On the far side of the cooking fires he saw his friend, Old Indian, and Sky Fire speaking to one another in very agitated voices. Kincade felt they kept glancing his way, but perhaps the laughing children had made him self-conscious. Sky Fire towered head and shoulders above Swift Raven, but the wrinkled octogenarian was not intimidated. He was speaking with equal anger and force. He stood as tall as he could and held his chin high, looking directly into Sky Fire's eyes. Kincade caught a glimpse of what Swift Raven must have looked like as a young man. Sky Fire shook his fist and Swift Raven, too, clenched his fingers as if ready to strike. Then he abruptly turned his back and proudly stalked away.

"I wonder if their argument was about me? Probably not. I'm just a little boy. Why would they fight over me?"

CHAPTER 15

NEXT MORNİNG WHEN a touch behind his ear awakened Kincade he looked, not into the smiling face of Old Indian, but the stern countenance of Sky Fire. Kincade jumped to his feet. The big Indian told him in a deep, gruff, unintelligible voice to put on his moccasins and come outside. He pointed to the stream where the young boys bathed and gave an order. Kincade realized he was to go there alone. He didn't mind. Old Indian had showed him what to do. Sky Fire strode off in the opposite direction toward the men's bathing pool.

On the stream bank, Kincade pulled off his clothes and jumped in with a splash. "I'm Kincade," he shouted – "Kincade!" Several of the boys shouted back, "Kincade! Kincade!" Soon all were calling his name. Together they laughed as the name 'Kincade' echoed back and forth. The strangeness had vanished. The Indian boys welcomed this newcomer into their village.

Everything went well until Wil arrived. He had not been given new clothes and he pulled off his dirty coveralls and jumped naked into the water. He made no effort to wash himself - only to attack Kincade. He started by pushing him down and then splashing water into his eyes until he could hardly see. Once Kincade was on his feet, Wil went under the water to pull his legs out from under him and Kincade went down again. He staggered as he got up and

Wil began to push and shove him backwards. Kincade wanted to run but Wil would not let him escape. Wil's eyes gleamed. "Fraidy-cat, fraidy-cat!" he chanted.

Kincade decided he must fight back, but Wil was an inherent bully and Kincade was not. His punches were easily dodged. When Wil held his brother's head under the water for a dangerously long time, an older boy had seen enough. He tackled Wil. Kincade came up sputtering. The Indian boy noticed the scars on Kincade's right bicep, carved there by Archibald Logan. He then turned to look at Wil's arm and saw similar marks. Returning his eyes to Kincade, the boy brought his two hands together and crossed left and right index fingers. He looked at Kincade questioningly. Kincade nodded. He and Wil were brothers.

The Indian boy understood. He pointed, and in a strange but recognizable command, ordered Wil to leave. "Didn't want to come anyhow!" was Wil's retort. Then he called back to Kincade, "Next time I'll drown you!"

Kincade regretted Wil's bad behavior, even though he had done nothing wrong himself. These Indian boys had been friendly and now perhaps they would shun both him and his brother. He started to leave, but the older boy took his hand and led him back. Bending down to the water, the boy cupped his hands into a bowl, filling it with water. He looked mischievously at Kincade, and threw the water into his face. The Indian boy laughed good-naturedly. Kincade laughed in return, splashing the boy back. Everything was still all right. The Indian boys accepted Kincade for who he was, not for the behavior of his brother. They had been taught by their elders that each and every thing on the Earth was unique unto itself.

No one ever awakened Kincade any more. It had been fun to open his eyes and find Old Indian inviting him to start a new day. But Sky Fire's look was a command ordering him to get up. It was impossible to be cheerful with Sky Fire. So when Pretty Butterfly left before dawn to start the fire for the morning meal, he would crawl out of his sleeping robe and follow her.

Kincade liked to sit cross-legged at the entrance of the tepee and listen to the birds voicing their wakefulness. Pretty Butterfly looked like a spirit shadow as she floated in the darkness. They said nothing to one another. The sky gradually grew rosy, the crisp air grew warmer. What would this day hold for him? He hoped Old Indian would come get him and they would do something special. When he finally saw other boys headed for the bathing pool, he joined them. That was always a good way to begin a new day. Wil never came again.

Sky Fire treated Kincade like a possession – not a person. And he was very jealous. Both men and women avoided Kincade rather than face Sky Fire's wrath. Swift Raven was the only defiant one. He made Kincade a small bow and was showing him how to place an arrow and release it when Sky Fire came upon them. He broke the bow and arrow across his knee and threw the pieces in the fire. Kincade had to laugh when his friend, Old Indian, made him an even better bow and arrow but kept them safe in his own tepee.

Old Indian made Kincade a wingbone whistle. Sky Fire grabbed it from the boy's lips and threw it in Pretty Butterfly's bowl of soup. After her husband had stomped off, she fished it out, licked it, and handed it back to Kincade with a smile. She always showed respect for Sky Fire in his presence, but frequently did things her way when alone.

As possessive as he was, Sky Fire spent very little time with Kincade. He was an important warrior and passed hours with the headmen and councillors in the largest tepee. A few times the edges were rolled up and tied so that everyone could listen to their decisions. Kincade saw them pass around a long pipe, some smoking it, others just touching it to their lips.

Sky Fire spent hours riding the big, black horse in the intricate maneuvers of the buffalo hunt. He also rode it in races against other tribesmen, always winning. He tested his weapons and made new ones. Whenever the elder tribesmen decided on a raid, braves from the neighboring village would join in. Sky Fire would be in the lead. Sometimes they attacked their enemies, more to steal horses than to kill. To touch a fallen armed foe was considered the greatest bravery. Avenging raids to atone for the death of a tribal member were more deadly and the braves returned with scalps hung from their lances and horses' tails. These raids always took many days. When Swift Raven saw Sky Fire ride away on the black war horse he would quickly find Kincade and they would do special things together.

Kincade and Swift Raven would walk in the forest. They would find a spot to simply sit, to be quiet, and watch. They talked only in whispers, and Kincade was surprised that he understood most of what Swift Raven shared, even though the language was unintelligible.

Swift Raven taught Kincade the names of the animals they saw. A fat, brown porcupine waddled across their path, his quills flat against his back. Swift Raven whispered, "Pahin," and the porcupine turned its back to the sound. It raised its quills and lashed out with his tail. "Old Indian, we'd better move away," Kincade said. Swift Raven gestured that the animal could not throw his quills, only strike with them. He also pointed to the colored designs sewed on Kincade's moccasins. The boy realized they were made from the dyed quills of a pahin.

Another day when the two were hidden, a black and white, flat-footed animal trotted nearby. "Maka!" Swift Raven said. Quickly he grabbed the creature by the head and tail and was ready to smack its exposed belly against a tree to kill it, for the skin was deeply prized. "Old Indian! No!" Kincade protested loudly. Swift Raven laughed and threw it as far as he could as the two ran in the opposite direction. Evidently the skunk survived its fall because the air was drenched with a stink unlike anything Kincade had ever experienced.

Swift Raven talked, not only with words, but with gestures and pantomime. Gradually Kincade started to understand him more and more, even to the point of using the Indian words himself. Their clothes were made from hide of the deer they watched feeding in a meadow. "Tahca," Swift Raven told him. Sometimes prairie dogs sat by their holes barking at them. "Dispiza," the old Indian told him. The bounding rabbits were "mastincala." The imperial eagle soaring overhead, whose feathers were dearly prized, was "wambi". Kincade always repeated the word and tried to remember, but most of all he remembered the funny antics of Swift Raven as he mimicked the animals and birds and crawling creatures. Kincade wanted these special days to continue forever. However, if they got close to the village and Kincade saw Sky Fire's horse tied outside the tepee signaling he had come back, the two would return on different paths.

Whenever Kincade saw Wil he felt pity. Apparently he belonged to no special Indian for he slept in a large tepee with about ten other children. He ate whatever he could beg from the various women. His overalls were torn and filthy. He had been given a shirt without fringe and moccasins with no decoration. Wil was not welcome to join the games played by the other boys because they had learned quickly that he disrupted their fun. He showed his resentment by pushing and shoving them whenever possible. Kincade liked many of the boys and they liked him. Sky Fire was not a father figure, but neither had Archie been. Pretty Butterfly was kind and gave him food and shelter, and he had a very special friend whom he called Old Indian. Wil wandered alone, belonging nowhere and to no one.

One day after Kincade saw a particularly ugly incident between Wil and some Indian boys he said to Old Indian, "Wil isn't liked, is he."

"No."

"That's too bad. The boys are very nice to me."

Old Indian smiled at his innocence. "As you behave towards others, they will behave towards you. Remember that."

Kincade considered the answer. "I will remember because I want people to like me."

"Then they will."

He paused and looked to Old Indian for another answer that bothered him. "I wish Wil would like me."

Swift Raven sadly shook his head. "That is his problem. Don't make it yours by hating him in return."

Kincade smiled. "Thank you, Old Indian. I'm glad I can tell you anything."

CHAPTER 16

CORPORAL ARCHIBALD LOGAN stood at attention before Captain Brooker. He kept his eyes straight forward and his mouth firm. He had gone into prison a brutal man; he had come out a hardened criminal. He had been listening with contempt to this command to find his sons. He didn't give a damn if the Indians boiled them alive and ate them with salt and pepper. But he needed money to fulfill his plans to acquire ill begotten wealth in San Francisco. As he listened more carefully, he decided this assignment wasn't too bad. Maybe he'd pass through a small town with an easy bank to rob; maybe a stage with miners' gold could be held up; maybe a wealthy rancher could be shot and his house looted. Then he'd hightail it to California. All these possibilities for getting money intrigued him, for at this moment he had only two dollars in his pocket.

"Yes Sir. I understand completely."

"Privates Marcos and Mulligan will accompany you and you'll have two pack horses. Also the Indian trader will come along to serve as your interpreter. Do you know him?"

"Yes, Sir. His name's White Paw Willie, I believe."

"I am assigning you only a small contingent." Logan flinched.

Brooker continued. "I'm doing this for three reasons. First, you will appear less hostile to the Indians. Second, you will not be tempted to append your orders."

Brooker stopped and said nothing further, looking squarely into Logan's eyes. That stare lasted for over a minute. Logan swore to himself that he saw menace in the Captain's eyes.

Brooker finally broke the silence. "And the third reason, Corporal Logan, is I don't trust you."

If he had not been the Captain of the Fort, Logan would have leapt at his throat. "Corporal, let me make this clear. Your only duty is to find your sons. You are not to commit acts of violence. Do you understand?"

"Yes, Sir." His voice was firm but his teeth were grinding.

"You are to leave tomorrow. Inquire at all the Indian villages within a hundred mile radius. You are to enter every Indian village bearing a white flag. The Indians have come to accept and trust this symbol of our peaceful intentions. In no way are you to violate their trust. Do you understand?"

This order was almost too much for Logan to swallow. Peace? Trust? What did savages know about either? Only his desire to get this mission over with and get to San Francisco made him answer, "Yes, Sir."

"You have no more than six months, Corporal. Hopefully in six weeks you will be able to return the boys to your wife." Logan grimaced but Brooker continued. "Would you like to see your wife before you go?"

Logan hesitated. "Only if that's an order, Sir."

The Captain felt a personal disgust for the soldier in front of him. "Your decision entirely. You are dismissed."

"Yes, Sir." Logan saluted, did an about face, and left the room. "A hundred mile radius," he was thinking. "There's bound to be some action within a hundred miles." Calming himself after being dressed down by his superior, Logan chuckled. "Wonder if Marcos and Mulligan would like to be in on it? No, I'll be better off alone." He went to the barracks to pack a duffle bag for what could be a long trip. He had no intention of seeing Angela – ever.

*   *   *   *   *   *

The summer season was closing. No buffalo had been spotted within an easy distance to transport the harvest back to the camp. The Shaman had danced and performed the rites of "calling" the buffalo. His medicine bundle held powerful talismans. Inside was a perfectly round hair ball taken from the stomach of a bull which had licked its fur, and three red stones shaped like buffalos. The headmen and councillors had joined the Shaman in the largest tepee and smoked the long pipe. Now everyone waited, for the survival of the tribe depended on the buffalo – food and clothing, lodging and weapons, utensils and tools, even games. Swift Raven told Kincade, "We will be held in a long and bitter grasp if the buffalo do not come before the snows."

Then on a bright fall morning a scout galloped into the circle of tepees bringing the long awaited news. A massive herd of buffalo was on the move in their direction. Twenty seasoned hunters immediately began to organize. They would be joined by fifty from the neighboring village.

"Will you go, Old Indian?" Kincade asked.

"My killing days were over long ago."

"Can I go? Just to watch maybe?"

"No. But there will be plenty for both of us to do here."

The camp became a flurry of activity – both men and women preparing for the hunt. The braves would do the killing. Skinning, butchering, and transporting were women's work. Pretty Butterfly sent Kincade back and forth to ready her two horses and two dogs for the drags. Sky Fire checked his weapons, and gave special attention to the black horse. He didn't mind if Kincade watched as long as he didn't ask questions or get in the way. He paid no attention when Kincade turned to Swift Raven to find out about things that were going on.

The hunt succeeded beyond the tribe's greatest hopes. Great rejoicing filled both villages. A nighttime dance brought all the hunt participants to sing and recount their experiences around a huge fire throwing light far into the darkness.

All knew that the processing of all the body parts must begin immediately. Early the next morning hides were being pegged to the ground for tanning into rawhide or buckskin; tendons were being soaked and then twisted for cordage, bow strings, and sewing thread; hoofs and necks were boiled in paunches until there was a sticky soup for the gluing of bows and arrows; long hairs of the buffalo were being braided for the horses' jaw-thongs; bones were set aside for implements and tools. Kincade was kept busy hanging slender strips of meat on drying racks.

While the women were hard at work on these many tasks, the men had their horses and weapons to inspect. None of the animals had been crippled or gored in this hunt, for which all could be thankful since a tribe's wealth was counted in horses. Men checked the strength of their bows and strung new strings. They checked the straightness of the arrow shafts that had been pulled from fallen beasts and arrowheads were sharpened.

Kincade saw that Sky Fire strutted around to brag how many hides were being hung outside his tepee and how few arrows he had needed to bring down his kills. The boy knew that the man was, indeed, a great hunter and warrior. But his prideful boasts and arrogance seemed to tarnish his accomplishments. Kincade much preferred the quiet power and confidence exuded by Old Indian. His quiet power was a dazzling beacon to Kincade, teaching the boy another of life's lessons: less is often more.

The time of rejoicing over the successful hunt and completion of labor was followed by days of depression. The neighboring village was moving to a better winter site. This area could not sustain so many families during the cold time when nothing grows and game either hides or sleeps. Relatives and friends would probably not see one another until the next summer encampment. When all drags were loaded and the leaders had formed up the long procession, one family did not follow the tribe south. Instead the woman raised their tepee in Sky Fire's circle.

The woman was Pretty Butterfly's sister, Laughing Maiden - Ehawee. She was in the last stages of pregnancy with her third child. She had delivered her second son while the tribe was on the move, going alone into the bushes and bringing forth the baby in time to rejoin the group before the end of that day. She did not choose to do this again for the preceding eight months had given her considerable concern. The husband was a kind and obliging man, so it was agreed they would live close by Pretty Butterfly in case help was needed with the delivery.

Sky Fire welcomed the family for the man was a famous scout whose deeds were known throughout the territory. His name was Ozuye Najin – Standing Warrior.

CHAPTER 17

THERE WAS A knock on Captain Brooker's door. "Come in." Harry stepped into the office and saluted smartly. "Ah, Harry. Congratulations on your promotion. It's well deserved, but I shall miss having you here with me at the Fort."

"Thank you, Sir." The young man seemed uncomfortable. "May I speak with you, Sir, on a personal matter?"

"Of course, Harry. Please sit down. Would you like a cigar?"

"No thank you, Sir. I don't smoke."

"Do you mind if I do?" The Captain took a cigar from a humidor.

Harry didn't think it was his place to tell the Captain what to do. "Whatever is your pleasure, Sir."

The Captain bit off the tip, smelled the length, and lit a match. "What personal matter brings you to me, Harry? Are you considering marriage with your increase in pay?"

"Hardly, Sir." He smiled, feeling more at ease. "It's about a certain responsibility that I'll be leaving behind when I go, and I don't know what to do about it."

"What responsibility is that, Harry? Speak up, and I'll try to resolve your dilemma." The Captain drew heavily on the cigar.

The young man fidgeted in the chair, searching for the words that he'd been practicing all day. Deciding it was best just to blurt out the problem, he said, "I've felt very sorry for Mrs. Logan living way out there with no one but her two little boys and even they's gone now. She's a right nice lady, and…." He hesitated. "Her husband didn't treat her very well."

"So I've heard." The Captain puffed on his cigar. "But he did send her supplies regularly, didn't he?"

"That's my dilemma, Sir. Capta…..Corporal Logan always stole those groceries from the commissary and then paid me – not much, you understand - to deliver them. I knew he was stealing things, but golly, Sir, he was the Captain! Who was I supposed to report him to?"

Captain Brooker contemplated the smoke rings he was blowing. "Go on, Harry."

"Well, when he was demoted and sent away there was no one to take Mrs. Logan her groceries and mail. So I've…" He swallowed hard. "I've been buying what she's needed with my own salary. She doesn't suspect and I wouldn't want her to. But she's such a nice lady…" Harry hung his head as if he'd been doing something very wrong.

The Captain blew one last ring and then ground out the cigar in the ashtray. "That was a very kind thing for you to do, Harry. And you're worried that when you leave no one will care for her – am I right?"

"That's right, Sir."

"Perhaps Mrs. Brooker and I should take a little drive out there tomorrow and see how Mrs. Logan is faring. Don't you worry yourself any more, Harry. I will see that she doesn't go without."

"And, Sir, will you please take any mail from her sister. That's about the only thing that cheers her up nowadays."

"Glad you mentioned it." The Captain stood and shook Harry's hand. "You're a fine young man, Harry, and a credit to the army. You can go to your new assignment without a worry in the world – except perhaps getting along with your new Commanding Officer."

Harry stood and saluted. "Thank you, Sir." He turned to go and then looked back. "I'm going to miss Mrs. Logan, Captain Brooker." He closed the door behind him.

*   *   *   *   *   *

When Angela saw the Brooker buggy coming down the lane she jumped from the porch chair and ran to meet them. "Captain, Mrs. Brooker!" she shouted. "You've had news from Archie! He's found Kincade and will bring him home any day now!" She paused, realizing what she had just said. "Wil too, of course."

The Captain stepped from the buggy and gave his hand to his wife. "No, dear lady. I'm afraid not. I've heard nothing from your husband since he left three months ago. We just decided to take a little jaunt and see how you're faring." Both of the Brookers were shocked at the emaciated, unkempt woman who was barefoot and wore a bedraggled dress.

When Angela heard this she wilted like a flower on a grave. Then she tried to compose herself. "That's very kind of you. Please come in."

Mrs. Brooker retrieved a basket from the buggy. "I've brought a fresh coffee cake and some English tea. If you'll boil some water, my dear, we'll enjoy refreshments."

"That's very kind of you, Mrs. Brooker." Her tone was lifeless.

"Please call me Harriet. And may I call you Angela?"

"Yes, Ma'am." She led them back to the house and ushered them inside.

The scene was shocking.   Harriet wondered if anything had been done since the boys were kidnapped. Dirty dishes were everywhere. The bedclothes were rumpled and gray. Dust clung to all the furnishings and the floor had mud tracks from the last rain. Angela made no apology. She robotically lit the wood in the stove and put on the tea kettle. Then she looked for some cups and small plates which she had to rinse before setting them on the table.

The Captain was at a loss for something to say, and then he remembered the letter and pulled it from his pocket. "Harry asked me to give you this. It's from your sister, I believe."

Angela nodded, but took it without any reaction.   Harriet thought, "Poor darling! What can we do to help?"

The kettle boiled and Angela rose to pour the water into a chipped teapot without saying a word. Harriet wiped a used knife on her handkerchief and cut the coffee cake, putting the slices on the plates. "Would you like to read your letter now, dear?   The Captain and I won't mind."

"You're very kind. I think I will." Angela opened the envelope, but it just lay in her lap as she sipped her tea and slowly ate the coffee cake.

Harriet gave her husband a glance and then made a bold suggestion. "Angela, Harry tells us that you and your sister are very close. Perhaps it would be a good idea if you would go stay with her for awhile. Winter will be here before you know it and it would not be wise for you to be here all alone."

Angela jerked up. "Surely Archie will be back before winter."

"Maybe, maybe not," the Captain said. "You must seriously consider an alternative."

"But, Captain, I must be here when Archie brings Kincade back. I mustn't be off somewhere. He'll need his mother after all these terrible months with the savages. I can't go anywhere!"

"As soon as I get any word that they're on their way to the Fort, I'll let you know. Or better yet, I'll bring the boys to you at your sister's as soon as they arrive."

Angela looked doubtful. Harriet took her hands. "What if you were to get sick this winter out here all by yourself? What if you run out of wood for the stove or get snow bound? You must take care of yourself so the boys will have a strong and healthy mother when they return."

"Hmm," was all Angela said.

"I'm sure your sister would love to have you."

"She did suggest it a long time ago." Angela looked at the letter in her lap. She slowly took out the single sheet of paper. She read aloud in a soft voice. "Dearest sister. I absolutely insist that you come live here with me. We need one another in this time of fear and hope. I will come and get you as soon as I hear you agree. Please, dearest. I know you are grieving and to hold you in my arms is the only way I can help. I love you, Agnes."

Angela folded the page and put it back in the envelope. She

looked at Harriet and then at the Captain. "It's rather strange that her suggestion comes at the same time as yours." She paused to consider, and to silently agree that she must keep her health strong for Kincade's safe return. "Yes, I suppose it is best." She straightened her posture. "I will accept your advice and my sister's invitation. I will leave here." Looking around the soddy, she sighed. "Would it be asking too much for you to wire my sister that I'll be ready in a week?"

"I'm very glad you've made this decision, Mrs. Logan. I'll have the telegrapher at the Fort send your message as soon as we return. You can give me that envelope and I'll use Agnes's return address."

Angela clutched the letter to her breast as if even the envelope was precious. "No, Captain, I'll write it down for you." She rose and found a slip of paper and a pencil.

"I'll tell your sister that you'll be ready to leave Wednesday afternoon of next week. I will find someone to take your animals while you're away."

"You both are very kind," Angela repeated. She wasn't sure if she was relieved or distressed. It didn't matter. Others were making the decisions and she hadn't the strength to make them herself. It would be so good to feel Agnes's arms around her again.

CHAPTER 18

I N SPITE OF the cold and snow, the occasional blizzards and ice storms, winter was a good and happy time in the Indian village. Everyone had a warm robe. Adults' were of wooly buffalo hide. The children's were made from fluffy buffalo calf skins. Babies in cradleboards were snuggled down in rabbit fur. The women wore leggings under their knee-length skirts. Men who went bare-chested in summer put on shirts that their wives had laboriously decorated with colored quills.

Pretty Butterfly and her sister, Laughing Maiden, piled brush and timber around their tepees to keep out the cold. They had stacked a mountain of firewood nearby and also bark from cottonwood trees for the horses should there be a shortage of fodder before spring. They broke a hole in the ice and brought back full water sacs which hung inside their tepees. Kincade joyfully helped them with all these duties.

The delivery of Laughing Maiden's baby went without complication the very week that she raised her tepee close to Pretty Butterfly's. The baby was a smiling little girl. They named her Aponi, for this rare butterfly had been seen on the day of her birth. Pretty Butterfly was delighted with a name so similar to her own. She loved having her sister's three children visit her tepee for she had never had little ones of her own. That was the reason Sky Fire had brought her Kincade for a son, but something had been lacking in their relationship. Perhaps it was Kincade's fault for he still dreamed of a woman with fair skin and brown hair who sat in a chair on a porch and sang a Happy Song. A woman he called Mama. Pretty Butterfly didn't blame herself or the little boy. If she blamed anyone it was Sky Fire who had made no effort to act as a father. But that was a thought she mentioned to no one – not even Laughing Maiden.

There was always work for women. The dead of winter changed nothing in their responsibilities. The Indians wore out their moccasins at an alarming rate and the making of new ones took hours of sewing with awl and sinew. Winter was also a time to make new shirts and leggings. If quilling was to be added, the making took longer, but no woman would want another's husband to outshine her own brave's wardrobe. Kincade sat cross-legged in the tepee watching the dexterity of Pretty Butterfly's fingers. He was proud that she was acknowledged the best quiller in the tribe.

Winter saw the men staying in the circle of tepees rather than leaving on long raids. The scout, Standing Warrior, found deer and elk at a close distance so hunters could return the same day with game which the women easily dressed and cooked.

Everyone's humor was lifted by playing games which they had no time for in the summer months. Old persons too aged to do anything but the simplest tasks found companionship in small groups for betting their meager possessions on a toss or a guess.

The largest tepee was a gathering place for both men and women to play the moccasin game. Sky Fire was the leader, placing a small bone and six overturned moccasins before him. The bone was tucked under one and he rapidly switched the moccasins back and forth in a bewildering sequence. Bets were placed as to which moccasin hid the bone. Sky Fire flipped over each until the bone was finally revealed. The winners and losers paid off their bets and shouted that the game be played again. Kincade carefully watched and was always sure he could guess correctly, but he confessed, "Old Indian, I am happy that I have nothing to bet for I am always wrong."

On sunny days the tribe found outside amusement. The men made a track of hard-packed snow and flung arrows gliding toward a distant target. Sky Fire and his brother-in-law, Standing Warrior, were keen competitors. Women would take their turn, pushing a ball with a stick along the slippery path. The most excitable were the children who had sleds made of buffalo ribs. They scooted and yelled down the icy course until cold drove them inside to the tepee fires. Kincade had the best sled but kept it a secret from Sky Fire because Old Indian had made it for him.

When the wind howled and the snow whirled, as many Indians as possible congregated in the big lodge, their bodies adding warmth to the fire in the central pit. Others gathered in family tepees. It was story telling time, the recounting of traditions and legends which were forbidden to be told in the summer months. Anyone who did so could be turned into a hunchback.

Although there were several story tellers, everyone's favorite was Swift Raven. His gyrations and pantomimes, mimicry and tomfoolery held everyone spellbound or laughing with glee. Kincade would sit between Pretty Butterfly and Laughing Maiden with her children by her side. But he always felt that Old Indian was performing especially for him. Kincade now understood nearly every word that the octogenarian spoke, and those he didn't catch were easily understood by the dramatic presentation.

Kincade's favorite stories were about Iktomi. The Trickster could talk with animals who could talk back to him. He was always trying to trick them, but usually he was the one who got tricked. "Old Indian, please waddle like a duck, or swish your tail like a wolf, or scamper like a chipmunk!" Kincade would shout – much to the delight of both young and old.

The tale Kincade would remember for the rest of his life was the story of Wakan Tanka, the Great Mystery, making the Seven Directions: the Place of the Sunrise, the Place of Summer, the Place of the Sunset, and the Place of Winter. He took these four and put the Sky above and the Earth below. But he had one more direction – the Seventh. It was the most powerful for it contained the True Knowledge Of The Spirit. He needed to hide it for humans would want its power. Because the animals were wise, Wakan Tanka asked them where to put the Seventh Direction. Eagle suggested he put it in the sky. Bear thought it should be hidden in a dark cave. Fish thought the deepest sea. The Great Mystery declined these places knowing that man could one day fly to the sky, and dig deep into the earth, and reach the depths of the ocean. Finally Mole came up with the answer which Wakan Tanka thought was perfect. The Seventh Direction – True Knowledge of The Spirit - was placed in every person's heart. Wakan Tanka knew that one of the most difficult places for a person to see is into his own heart. Kincade thought a lot about that, and even though he was only a little boy he promised himself that one day he would look into his heart and find a person there who would recognize the True Knowledge of His Spirit. Far into Kincade's future, that promise would come true. Her name would be Josephine.

Spring did not come slowly. It pounced like a playful puppy, bursting the leaves onto the trees, the babble back to the stream, the warmth into the sunlight. Animals were emerging from winter hibernation and birds were returning from their southern homes. Everyone in the village stepped spritelier and the chatter of the women promised hope for a bountiful year ahead.

Spring brought the arrival of a newscarrier from their sister village which had passed the winter in a more favorable location. All the people clustered to hear about their friends and family but none more eagerly than Standing Warrior and Laughing Maiden. Yes, the tribe would be returning here after the next moon. Yes, the newscarrier would return with the word that Standing Warrior and Laughing Maiden would once again move their tepee to this larger group. There were so many personal messages to pass on to the excited listeners that the newscarrier was breathless before he got around to telling of the White men who had come to the village bearing a white flag of peace.

"Three soldiers and an Indian trader who can speak our language came seeking two White boys who were kidnapped by our people many moons ago." Sky Fire looked at Pretty Butterfly but his face held no expression. "They will take the boys back to their White mother. These men have been traveling from one village to another, but no one so far has seen or heard of them. These may be the boys you have here. They say they will trade for the boys but I don't know what they will offer."

The newscarrier looked around but saw only men and women listening to him. "They will be here tomorrow for we left at the same time, but I can travel more swiftly than they."

This bit of news set in motion a destiny for Kincade that only the Great Spirit could conceive... a destiny for the boy which would be stewarded by one person: Old Indian.

Swift Raven stepped away from the crowd and made his way back to his tepee. He had never had a son. He was not going to give up this little White boy who had captured his heart.

The entire village was fast asleep. Kincade had spread his robe between Sky Fire and Pretty Butterfly but was touching neither. He was dreaming again of the lady with the fair skin and brown hair when he felt a soft touch behind his ear. He opened his eyes and there was his friend Old Indian standing over him. He gently pinched Kincade's lips between his fingers, signaling that the boy should make no sound. He silently slipped out the tepee door and Kincade followed.

At a distance, Swift Raven's horse stood ready to pull a fully loaded drag, the long tepee poles protruding far behind. There was also a pack dog with bundles on a smaller drag. Swift Raven mounted the horse and indicated that Kincade should ride the dog. Like specters they disappeared from the village and into the forest. The moon rose and a coyote howled. They spoke not a word to one another. Kincade did not question why this was happening. He felt it was enough that they were going together – wherever that might be.

This night began a change of everything…

CHAPTER 19

S KY FIRE WAS certain that Kincade and Wil were the boys they were looking for.

"Kimimela Weeko," he shouted. "Where is the boy Kincade? He must be here to meet the White men."

"I haven't seen him, my husband."

"Then where is the other one?"

"I haven't seen him, my husband."

"Is that all you can say?" Thinking, as he had a hundred times before, how worthless the woman was, Sky Fire stormed off to inquire of others the whereabouts of the boys.

Soon he came back holding a reluctant Wil by the arm. "Where is your brother? Where is your brother?" he kept repeating. But Wil didn't understand for he had never learned one word in the Indian language.

"Quit yelling at me!" he replied, switching his expression back and forth from sullen to angry. Sky Fire was furious, but it was not the Indian custom to strike a child. It was believed that hitting only drove in the naughtiness. So Sky Fire planted the boy just outside the big tepee and let him know by gestures that he was not to go away.

"Kincade has fled," Sky Fire told Pretty Butterfly in his deep, gruff voice. "I have searched everywhere."

She tried to sooth his rising temper. "Perhaps Kincade doesn't want to return to his White mother. Perhaps he would prefer to continue living here."

Sky Fire accepted that idea. "I shall tell the White men that he once was here but has run away. We don't know where."

The headmen and councillors met in the big tepee before the White men arrived. It was important to impress them with their appearance, demeanor and wisdom. They bedecked themselves in their war bonnets and grizzly claw necklaces. They solemnly smoked the long pipe of truth and discussed how best to bargain with these strangers.

Corporal Logan was in the lead carrying the white flag as they rode into the circle of tepees. It had not been a congenial foursome. White Paw Willie spit tobacco every ten seconds, wiped his juice-stained beard with a dirty hand, and said things which could not possibly be of any interest to Archibald Logan. Privates Marcos and Mulligan had snickered behind his back about his being a jailbird. The only time he had liked them was when he won all their traveling stipends. Then he bragged about becoming a big time gambler in San Francisco. The commission was for a six month search and that time had almost ended. Find the boys or not, Logan was headed for California after this one last village.

The four stopped in front of what was obviously the council tepee and dismounted. The elders, braves, and advisors came out. Among them was the scout, Standing Warrior. He took one long look at Corporal Logan and immediately hurried from the circle.

His horse could be heard leaving the village at a fast gallop. No one questioned his abrupt departure for people were always free to come and go as they pleased.

"We come to find two White boys," White Paw Willie said in the Indian language. "You got 'em?"

Logan was staring at the boy standing by the tepee, his head down. He hadn't seen his sons for two years. Could this be one of them? He strode over and tore the boy's sleeve from his shirt. There, like a cattle brand, were the letters "W" and "L".

"Wilson, I'm your father."

"I know who you are and I know how I got those marks on my arm." Logan hit him hard across the mouth and the Indians gasped.

"Where's your brother? Where's Kincade?"

"How should I know? I'm not his keeper." Again he was slapped.

Logan turned to White Paw Willie. "Ask where the other boy is." The trader did.

"They say he's run away. Don't know where to."

"Hell! Well, start the bargaining. I want to get out of here."

White Paw Willie stepped inside the tepee followed by the headmen and councillors. Corporal Logan stayed outside, keeping his grip on Wil. He could hear mumbling and arguing from within.

White Paw Willie finally came out. "They'll turn over the boy after they get one hundred wool blankets and an iron cooking pot for every tepee."

Logan guffawed. "Tell them to go to hell! They should pay me to take him off their hands."

White Paw Willie entered the tepee and talked some more. When he emerged all the leaders followed him. "They say one hundred blankets. Forget the iron pots."

Logan gave Wil a push into their midst. "They can keep him! I'll tell his mother they watched the bears eat him." He mounted his horse and was turning away when Sky Fire stopped him. He spoke to White Paw Willie in a deep, gruff voice. "What'd he say?" Logan wanted to know.

White Paw Willie spit tobacco and wiped his beard. "He said, you take him. They don't want him. He'd not make a good Indian."

"That's more like it. He'll ride double with you, Marcos." The private reached for Wil's hand and swung him up behind his saddle. "I hear one peep out of you, Wilson, and I'll tell Private Mulligan to shoot your head off." The five rode out of the circle. Marcos and Mulligan had kept their mouths shut during the negotiations, but they were glad to be starting back to the Fort. One kid was better than none.

Standing Warrior rode like the wind to the village he considered his home... the village that had wintered in a more favorable place than Sky Fire's... the village where three small Indian children once lived before being murdered by a White butcher named Archibald Logan.

He rode with every fiber of his being, to the village of Chief Brave Eagle...

CHAPTER 20

MULLIGAN AND MARCOS awakened in their bivouac camp and lay still, waiting for Corporal Logan to order them to make coffee so they could get on their way again. It was quiet for so long that both the privates stretched their necks to see what was wrong with their leader. Usually he was barking orders and kicking their butts before dawn. He was no where to be seen.

Mulligan whispered, "Where the hell is he?"

"You think he's taking a leak?"

"I'll bet you a month's wages that he's headed for California like he's been talkin' about doin'. Desertion wouldn't mean nothin' to that jailbird."

They looked at Wil who was still sleeping close by. "Didn't take the kid with him," Marcos commented. "What'll we do?"

Something was wrong. Logan's horse was there, but the Corporal had disappeared. The hair on Mulligan's neck stood up as if a storm were brewing. "Let's get out of here… get the kid back to the Fort. Those were our orders, and I say the sooner the better. Wake him up!"

*   *   *   *   *   *

Scout Standing Warrior and Chief Brave Eagle rode quickly, deliberately, but with the whispered silence of windwalkers. Since the murder of the Chief's three children, both men had experienced the darkest depths of their hearts, tortured by what they could have done or what they should have done. They knew countless days filled with remorse. Their nights were wakeful or else tortuous dreams consumed their sleep. Standing Warrior believed he had failed his Chief by not going on a relentless quest for the perpetrator of the crime. Brave Eagle felt he no longer deserved his name, as grief had robbed him of the strong leadership he was known for.

The two were haunted. The ghosts of the three children called out to them. Vengeance would be theirs one day, and that day had arrived. The scout had confirmed to his Chief that the principal soldier was, indeed, the murderer of his beloved children.

Driven as one, Standing Warrior and Brave Eagle easily followed the small group of soldiers now headed back to the Fort. They led a riderless horse on a rope. The two waited with the vigilance of horned owls until all the White men and the boy were asleep. They waited until the camp's fire shrank to glowing embers, then to smoke, followed by nothing at all. They crept forward.

Without making the slightest sound, Brave Eagle struck a mind-numbing blow to Corporal Logan, rendering him immediately unconscious. They did not drag him for fear the sound would awaken the others. By his arms and legs, the two carried Logan away from his men, over a rise, down and through a ravine to where their mounts waited. They tied a band of leather over his eyes and stuffed a gag in his mouth. He did not stir. Then they secured him belly down to the spine of the third horse. Silently they slipped onto the backs of their own steeds and rapidly disappeared into the blackness like winged predators.

As Archibald Logan slowly regained consciousness, he realized he was blindfolded. The taste in his mouth was disgusting. He recognized the smell coming from whatever had been jammed into his throat: urine. He had been lashed onto a horse now running at a breakneck gallop. His wrists had been tied to his feet, so he was wrapped under the horse's belly like a human cinch. Logan's skull was pounded by the hammering of the horse's powerful legs. His chin smashed into the horse's ribs, cracking his teeth, causing his tongue to be painfully chewed. Had it not been for the urine-soaked rag, he would have bitten it off by the repeated impacts of man to beast.

He could hear the pounding hooves of two more horses just ahead of his, but no words were exchanged between their riders. He was terrified. He knew these were not bandits. Despite the rattling of his body, Logan knew he was bareback. And he knew of only one breed that could ride at this speed without benefit of saddle and stirrup. He had been taken by Indians!

The race forward into blackness continued for what seemed an eternity. Logan's fear become monstrous as the horses crashed through brush, leapt into frigid waters that nearly drowned him, up onto wet banks that splattered and filled his wheezing nostrils with mud. The spine of the horse slammed into his gut, churning his stomach's contents into a regurgitated stew, choking his throat with vomit.

Logan was riding to his death. But what he didn't know was how excruciatingly gruesome his death would be.

CHAPTER 21

A T FIRST, LOGAN thought he imagined it. The pounding hooves of the three charging horses concealed the first hint. But now the sounds grew louder, confirming his worst imaginings.

Drums were beating. Men were chanting. Women trilling that strange sound reserved for exciting moments. His blindfold blocked any view, but Logan could smell a big fire. Their horses began to slow. The three had reached their destination.

Footsteps approached the lathered horses as the two riders slipped from their mounts. Strong hands cut away Logan's bonds. He was pulled from his horse, his hands re-lashed and he was roughly pushed forward towards the heat. Finally, his blindfold was torn away.

He found himself in the center of a circle of war-painted savages, dancing on pounding feet, many brandishing lances and knives. Women were waving long poles back and forth over their heads. Scalps floated from the ends like waving flags. This dance had an object and a meaning. Each member of Brave Eagle's tribe wanted to throw every bit of their being into the dance performed in honor of their Chief.

Corporal Archibald Logan realized he was at the threshold of unimaginable suffering. Logan was a coward to his core. He had never been so frightened in his life. He faced raging flames from an unchained and unleashed hellfire.

Four strong braves dragged Logan to the edge of the fire and pushed him to his knees. Brave Eagle stood in front of his people as a large war bonnet was placed on his head, its eagle feathers so numerous that they trailed to the ground, each feather signifying an enemy killed by his hands.

The Chief nodded to Standing Warrior. The scout stepped forward to face Logan, drawing a knife from a sheath at his waist. The drums sounded, their beat increased in speed and intensity. Logan whimpered, pleading for his miserable life. The scout placed his hand around Logan's throat, steadying the soldier's head as four braves held him in his kneeling position. With the skilled precision of his name, Standing Warrior took the sharpened tip of the blade to the top of Logan's skull. There, he pushed the tip through the hair and into the thin flesh of Logan's scalp, but not so deep as to penetrate the bone. He slowly drew the blade towards Logan's forehead, turned the tip to cross the brow, back again into the soldier's hair towards the crown of his head, finally returning the knife tip to connect with its starting place. Logan screamed at the excruciating pain.

Standing Warrior then placed the side of the knife parallel to Logan's skull, inserting the blade between scalp and bone. As he pushed, the flesh peeled away like ripe fruit. The scout released his grip on Logan's throat to grab the handful of loosened hair. The tribe's Shaman sang and the drums beat even louder. Women rattled gourds creating a discordant sound. Other braves raised bones with notches in them, dragging other bones across the indentations in a grating sound.

Standing Warrior turned to face Brave Eagle, his Chief and the father of Red Leaf, Yellow Horse and Little White Dove. He

raised his head back to howl like the wolf at the blackness overhead. In tribute, in revenge, he yanked his closed fist from Logan's
skull, raising it high above his own head. In his fist was Logan's
scalp. The scout's precision with the knife had deliberately not
killed the man, and his skeletal skull gleamed in the firelight as
blood ran down Logan's face.

The women stepped forward, dancing in concentric circles
around Standing Warrior and the kneeling Archibald Logan. In
groups of four to twelve, the women pressed their shoulders against
each other. At every stroke of the drums, they raised themselves
to their utmost height, hopping and sliding a short distance to the
left, singing all the time with the rest of the tribe.

Four of the women approached Standing Warrior. They held
a pole in their hands to which was attached a hoop. Feathers,
ribbons, beads and other trinkets adorned the hoop. The women
took Logan's scalp and secured it to the hoop with leather strips,
stretching the skin from edge to edge. Once done, Standing Warrior took the pole and walked forward to stand alongside Brave
Eagle. He turned to speak before the entire tribe, which fell completely silent.

As Archibald Logan babbled deliriously, Standing Warrior related his eye-witness account of the death of Brave Eagle's children at the hands of the soldier kneeling before them. The tribe
listened in a great hush as the fire crackled and sparks flew into the
black sky. The tale ended and all nodded as they understood fully
what Logan had done.

The Corporal looked into the face of Brave Eagle, sure that he
was about to be killed.

But no. The ritual had only begun.

CHAPTER 22

THE FOUR BRAVES pulled Logan to his feet. Standing Warrior walked forward, accepting a long leather rope from one of the women. He placed the rope around Logan's neck who imagined he was about to be hanged. But Standing Warrior knotted the rope to act as a leash rather than a noose. The scout then joined the four braves to face Brave Eagle.

The Chief nodded his approval. He turned his back on Logan and began to walk towards the high rock cliffs that surrounded the village. Standing Warrior followed at a respectful distance, trailed by the braves who led Logan like a leashed dog. A full moon had appeared over the rimrock, illuminating their way.

Brave Eagle knew that the predator would not be in her lair. Cougars hunted at night, and with the four kittens she had birthed three weeks ago, she would not return to her cave without the kill of a white-tailed deer.

The tribe held the Cougar in great respect, picking this particular valley for their village in order to be close to a beast so revered in their religion and culture. This female Cougar was one of the most magnificent Brave Eagle had ever seen. Her fur was a sleek gray-brown, her body over six feet long and tremendously muscular.

Brave Eagle had watched her swim, climb trees and leap horizontally and vertically equally well. He marveled at her hunting skills. She did not chase down her prey, but rather stalked and ambushed. Once, he had seen her leap over twenty feet onto a deer's back instantly killing the animal with one ferocious bite to the neck.

Her lair was reached through a tight canyon, up a headwall and into a cave tucked into a cliff. As the Indians approached with their captive, four cougar kittens could be heard mewing loudly deep in the recess, expecting their mother's return.

The cave was surrounded by the ghostly remains of an ancient bristlecone pine forest. Silhouettes of naked branches stretched like arms, frozen in the pose of a macabre death dance. Brave Eagle signaled to Standing Warrior and the four braves to drag Logan to the most sturdy trunk. It stood directly in front of the cave with one limb extended like a gibbet. The soldier wailed, crazed at the thought of what might happen next.

Chief Brave Eagle stood to one side as he signaled Standing Warrior to begin the ceremony they had planned. The scout first stripped the captive naked. He then removed a length of rope from his waist, lofting one end over the branch. He lashed the soldier's hands securely behind his back with the dangling rope. Using his considerable strength to pull, he raised Logan to suspend him in midair. The victim was screaming as the weight of his body almost tore his arms from their sockets.

Logan's ankles were then bound tighter and tighter, until the soldier was swinging like a trussed up carcass in a slaughter house. He lost control of his bowels.

Standing Warrior checked to make sure Logan could not free himself from the rope suspension. Then he turned to his Chief and they both nodded. Standing Warrior joined the four braves and they began their walk back to the village.

Brave Eagle was now alone with Logan. He waited for a message from the Wakanpi, invisible beings who exercised power and control over everything. Wafting clouds drifted in and out of the moonlight. Then he knew. The Chief untied the thong holding a medicine bag on his chest. Reaching inside the small pouch, he removed the Cougar fetish given him many moons ago by the Shaman, Man Of The Mysterious Voice. Holding the carved stone in one hand, Brave Eagle grasped his knife with the other. He brought it across his chest to carve a gash just above his beating heart. He and the Cougar would become as one – to share the same blood – to perform a human sacrifice as one entity. He pressed the fetish into his own blood and chanted, "In the east mountain, the Cougar comes alive. Drink the blood of the Cougar." Then he licked the stone clean.

Kneeling down, Brave Eagle placed the fetish at the feet of the dangling Archibald Logan who was oblivious to the ceremony. His mind had snapped and his terror had turned into whimpering gibberish.

Backing up, the Chief left the bristlecone pine forest and the four kittens who were mewing in chorus for the return of their Cougar mother.

That night, long after the tribe's fire had died out, the ghastly screams of a human being hideously torn apart, drifted across the Indian village. Brave Eagle stood before his lodge with eyes closed. His soul-mate, the Cougar, was acting for himself. When silence finally reclaimed the night, Brave Eagle walked to the smoldering ceremonial fire, retrieved the pole with Logan's scalp and jammed the shaft into the ground before his tepee.

Chief Brave Eagle opened the buffalo robe covering his lodge entrance, went inside and closed the hide behind him. His children were now avenged and could transcend into the Spirit World. He, as well as they, were finally at peace.

CHAPTER 23

MARCOS AND MULLIGAN turned Wil over to Captain Brooker, recounted the events of all their months away, and said that Corporal Logan had evidently deserted and gone to California. The Captain thanked them. "Will you please take this young man to my home, gentlemen. I believe my wife will be able to clean him up better than I could." The Captain then went directly to the telegraph office to send Angela Logan a wire: One boy found STOP Praise God STOP Will bring him to you within a week. STOP Warm regards from Harriet and Captain William Brooker.

Angela was beside herself with joy. "Agnes, Agnes, darling sister! Isn't it wonderful! My precious Kincade will be here in just a few days. Do I look well? He mustn't know I've been ill. Help me, Agnes. What shall we plan to eat? Everything Kincade likes. Apple pie is his favorite. Oh dearest, dearest sister. I have prayed for his return daily, over and over again. Now I only have a few days left to wait."

A buggy pulled up in front of Agnes's house. Angela straightened her hair and smoothed her dress. She was ready to rush outside when her sister stopped her. "Be a lady, Angela. After all he is Commander of the Fort." Agnes went to the door and ushered in the Captain and his wife, and hiding behind them was a boy.

"Come. Darling. Come to Mother. Don't be afraid." The boy stepped out and Angela screamed. "Wil! Oh my God, it's just Wil." She backed away, and looked at the Captain with resentful eyes. "If you could only bring me one of my sons, why did it have to be him!" She pointed to the scowling boy. "I want my Kincade – not him! Not Wil!" She burst into tears and ran from the room.

Harriet started to go after her, but Agnes held her back. "She had so hoped....."

The boy thrust out his chin. "Don't matter. I didn't wanna come here neither." He turned and went outside to sit on the porch steps.

"What shall we do?" the Captain asked Agnes. "Shall we leave him here or take him back?"

"Leave him, Captain. It may take her some time but I'm here. We'll manage, and thank you for bringing him."

The Brookers left. As the Captain went down the steps he patted the top of Wil's head. The boy brushed his hand away. "I ain't no sissy. I don't need them two old hags runnin' my life. And I hope Kincade got et by a bear when he run away."

*   *   *   *   *   *

Sky Fire kept expecting Kincade to return. But days went by and no sign of the boy. He became irritated, especially at his wife. "You said the boy was hiding because he preferred to stay with us!"

"I was only guessing."

"Women are supposed to supervise the children. A fine job you did! No telling where he is or what has happened to him. It's your fault that we don't have a hundred wool blankets!"

Sky Fire's accusations got the best of her. "Have you noticed that Kangee Kohana is also gone? His tepee, horse, dog – everything!"

Sky Fire's temper exploded. Swift Raven – his nemesis! "Why have you waited so long to tell me this? That old Indian was always trying to take my place with Kincade!"

Pretty Butterfly seldom got angry, but when she did she was like a wild cat. She threw the moccasins she had been making at her husband. "He did nothing that you couldn't have done yourself if you'd taken the time."

"You throw moccasins at your husband! Leave the tepee!"

"This is not your tepee. It is my tepee! The only things you own here are your clothes and your weapons! Kangee Kohana is a good old Indian who loves the boy."

"You take his side against me?

"I take the boy's side. I have lived with your cold indifference towards me. I know that if he had reached out to you, you would only have walked away."

"Kangee Kohana stole my son."

"No, he stole your pride."

"If a man steals my horse, I kill him. If a man steals my war bonnet and long pipe, I kill him. If a man steals my newly strung bow and quiver of fine arrows, I kill him. If a man steals my buffalo hide shield and lance with the scalps of my enemies, I kill him. Kangee Kohana steals my son, I will hunt him down and kill him." Sky Fire stormed out of the tepee, jumped on his black horse, and rode out of the circle of tepees. Pretty Butterfly had no doubt that he meant what he said.

A week later when he returned Sky Fire found only the skeleton poles of his tepee standing. The buffalo hide cover was gone. All the furnishings were gone. His personal belongings – his war bonnet and long pipe, his bow and quiver, his shield and lance, his clothing – had been placed outside the circle of poles where once the entrance to the tepee had been. Pretty Butterfly had divorced him. She had hitched the drags to her horses and her dogs and loaded them with her things. Her only possessions left behind were the tepee poles. She would not need them for she had chosen to become second wife to Standing Warrior. She joined her sister, Laughing Maiden, and the scout when they moved back to the neighboring village.

Pretty Butterfly smiled outwardly as her new life blossomed living with her sister.... smiled inwardly as the tendrils of her private revenge against Sky Fire took root.

For Kangee Kohana – Swift Raven - was their father.

PART THREE

CHAPTER 24

KINCADE HAD RIDDEN silently on the dog behind Swift Raven without ever questioning the reason for their journey into the night. The stars were
brilliant in the blackness. Swift Raven had told him stories of the
spirits of light high above and their march across the dark dome of
the sky. Now Swift Raven seemed to be following a secret pathway which the little spirits of light had made known to him. Kincade's drag-dog followed Swift Raven's drag-horse like a seasoned
beast of burden that it was.

It was not difficult for Kincade to stay awake even though he had
been roused from a deep sleep. The sounds through which they
traveled kept him alert, for he usually was fast asleep before night
creatures began their utterances. An owl hooted in questioning
cadence. A coyote howled and was answered by a multitude of
echoes. A raccoon bossed her little ones with a crisp trilling. There
was scurrying and rustling of unseen creatures in the tall grass.
There were bright eyes peering at them through tangled thickets.

When they stopped to let the animals rest and drink from a
small stream, Swift Raven asked, "Are you afraid?"

Kincade dipped his hand into the cold water. "I don't think so."
He slurped the good wetness and wiped his lips. "Are you afraid,
Old Indian?"

It was too dark for Kincade to see Swift Raven's smile. "I don't think so. But if I ever become afraid in the dark I tell myself that whatever I fear out there is just as afraid of me. We stay away from one another." Swift Raven stooped to scoop and drink. Then he stood. "I don't want you to fall off the dog. If you're getting sleepy you can ride with me."

The fascination of riding into the night had worn off and suddenly Kincade's eyes felt heavy. He held up his arms and Swift Raven swung him onto the horse, easily mounting behind him and putting his arms around the boy's waist. Kincade snuggled close. He had a faint recollection of falling asleep a long time ago in someone's arms who had light skin and brown hair. She was singing.

The drag animals plodded on. Swift Raven looked at the stars, listened to the night sounds, and smelled the childish freshness of a son he had never known before.

* * * * * *

Sky Fire was furious to have returned without the boy. When he first started out, their trail had been clear for half a day. Then suddenly Sky Fire could find no track or sign of the old Indian and Kincade. Swift Raven had once been a canny scout. The old Indian looked like a dried up piece of buffalo hide, but his instincts for deception were apparently as sharp as ever.

Sky Fire was a warrior - not a scout. He could kill man or beast once the prey had been spotted. But his eyes, ears, and nose were untrained for tracking. Swift Raven had eluded capture, and with him Kincade. So be it. Neither was worth his time.

Sky Fire returned to the village, prepared to carry on his life as before. But the life he had known had vanished, just as Swift Raven and the boy. Pretty Butterfly had divorced him in the most humiliating way! Long ago, Sky Fire had left his birth tribe to come to his wife's village, as was the custom. But now, Pretty Butterfly had destroyed his high status. Divorce by a woman was not common, especially by someone like Pretty Butterfly who had the respect of all in the village. Sky Fire must have done something unforgivable.

Previously, the warrior would have been greeted and welcomed home when returning from afar. But no longer. He had become an outcast.

Enraged, Sky Fire came to the center of the circle of tepees and beat upon his chest. "Let all who can hear my voice know I hold Kangee Kohana responsible for my misery." People stopped whatever they were doing and gathered to listen. Would he speak of the disappearance of Swift Raven? "Let all who can hear me know that the old Indian stole my son, Kincade. He is responsible for the disappearance of my wife, Kimimela Weeko. All that I value in this village has been despoiled. I will not rest until Kangee Kohana pays with his life for these injustices. Hear me, and know my pledge."

Sky Fire strode from the circle and rolled his few belongings into the buffalo robe which was part of his winter clothing. He then went to where captured horses were corralled. He chose an animal that he had once stolen from the Crow tribe, but had not yet trained for hunting buffalo. It was a placid beast and he easily tied his pack onto its back. He put the jaw-thong around its head. Then mounting his black stallion he led the second horse away from the village.

Sky Fire's outlook for the future had turned upside-down, but one goal was as clear as the morning sun - to find Swift Raven. Nothing would stop him from the revenge he swore would be his.

But where was he to go? How would he exist without a woman to make his moccasins and boil his meat? Then the answer struck him like a bolt of lightning. The news-carrier had spoken of renegade Indians in the area. These savages attacked their chosen enemies without mercy. They had scouts who could track a water snake over a bubbling pool. He would find these men. They would know how to live off the land. Sky Fire would become one of them. No, he would become their leader. They would aid him in his quest for vengeance. His days of tribal conformity were over. Sky Fire tasted the delicious sensation of freedom and eventual conquest.

*   *   *   *   *   *

For three days Swift Raven and Kincade traveled farther and farther away from the Indian village. Outwardly the old man always seemed to know where he was going but inwardly he was secretly looking for hiding places never before known to any man. Several times a day they stopped where there was a stream or spring to fill their water-sacs and let the animals rest. Whenever they felt hungry they chewed on dried meat and berries brought by Swift Raven. When the sun began its disappearing journey into the distance, Swift Raven would find a place to stop. They lit no fire for cooking and since the summer weather was upon them, a fire for warmth was unnecessary.

In the twilight hours Swift Raven would tell Kincade stories of the animal helpers. "Animals remember what humans forget," he would say. "Look to them for wisdom and you too can become wise. That is the Indian Way." When darkness overcame them they both lay down on Swift Raven's big buffalo robe. It had been so long since Kincade had slept with anyone beside him that at first he was afraid to turn over. But Swift Raven never pushed him away and soon he was snuggled up with his arm around the warm, wrinkled body.

On the fourth day Swift Raven came to a stop where a towering butte met tall aspen trees. A lively spring kept a shallow pool full before sending its waters tumbling across a grassy slope. He dismounted and walked back and forth, looking in all four directions. He then lifted Kincade to the ground. "We will live here."

"Forever and ever, Old Indian?" the boy asked.

"We only live one day at a time. We shall see how long those single days string together."

They began unloading the drags and spreading out the makings of a tepee just as Kincade had watched Pretty Butterfly do almost two years ago. "Old Indian, may I make the climb up the pins to fasten the two sides together?" he asked.

"Yes. You are the squirrel climbing the tree. I am only the blue-jay screeching instructions to you."

When the tepee had been erected and the water sacs filled, Swift Raven killed a rabbit. "Have you seen what is done now?" he asked the boy.

"Yes. Pretty Butterfly skinned it and pulled out everything we weren't going to eat. She threw that to the dogs. Then she put the rabbit on a long stick over the fire and kept turning it until it was brown and sizzling."

"Very good. I'm glad you watched so carefully because from now on that is your job. I kill the rabbit – you fix it to eat."

"Old Indian, that is women's work!" Kincade replied.

"Do you see any women?" The boy shook his head.

"I don't see any either." He handed Kincade the carcass.

"Someday can I kill the rabbit and you fix it to eat?"

"Someday, when your arrow can strike something besides a buffalo bag. Today it was my arrow."

"Did you bring my bow and arrow?" Swift Raven nodded. "Then I must learn how to shoot at a moving target like a rabbit. I will be a better hunter than a cook."

"But not tonight. Here is your skinning knife. Get to work. And when you are finished I will teach you how to make fire by twirling a stick in the Indian Way."

CHAPTER 25

THERE WERE ONLY two of them, one to teach and one to learn. But not just the essential tasks for daily living. Swift Raven was giving Kincade the understanding of Indian ways and beliefs. Hardly a day went by without a story or a ceremony to instill Indianhood into the boy – now seven years old.

"I must kill a deer, not only for its meat but for the hide which you will cure and soften and make into new moccasins for us both. We have only one pair left."

"May I shoot the deer? I'm getting better with my aim. I've killed two rabbits and one squirrel."

"If you see a deer the size of a rabbit or a squirrel I will let you kill it. If not, I will be the one to draw the bow." Kincade looked crestfallen. "There is something important that must be done before I shoot the deer and you will be the one to do it." Kincade perked up. "We must thank the deer for giving up his life for us. Without him we would go hungry and barefoot. We must promise him we will not use him wastefully. That is the Indian Way. Can you do that?"

"Will he hear me?"

"Of course. Remember, animals are smarter than humans and can understand us even if we don't always understand them. He will be pleased that we acknowledge his worth." Kincade was happy with his role.

"Old Indian, can I carry my bow and arrow when you go hunting – even if I don't shoot the deer?"

"Of course. Even great hunters do not always shoot their arrows but carry their weapon as a symbol of their place in the tribe. You will one day be a great hunter – perhaps of men if not animals. Always carry your weapon as a symbol of your status whether you shoot it or not."

Kincade listened and wondered. "A great hunter of men? What does that mean?" One day Kincade would remember Swift Raven's words and know what he had meant by carrying a weapon as a symbol of status.

"Hurry and get your bow and arrows or I shall be making a trail alone."

*   *   *   *   *   *

Soon after Sky Fire was divorced by Pretty Butterfly he had joined a band made up of fifteen renegades from ten different tribes, all related by family ties. These were young bucks who had rebelled against the traditions and ceremonies which elders expected them to honor. The arrival of White men gave them an excuse to vent their passions against unwanted and despised strangers. Sky Fire was older than any of them, and nearly as old as the elders the bucks detested. But instead of resenting his seniority they admired the many scalps hanging on his shield, his necklace of grizzly bear claws, the look of hatred and determination in his eyes, which far exceeded the combined wrath of the fifteen young braves. Sky Fire fueled the fury boiling within them. The fifteen not only accepted him, but made him their unquestioned leader.

Before Sky Fire's arrival their raids had been sporadic and hap-hazard – motivated as much by pent up energy as any purpose their twisted minds could justify. Just as Sky Fire had organized his tribe for buffalo hunts and avenging raids, he took command of the fifteen, ordering them to obey and act in any manner that suited him.

Sky Fire had a very specific and deliberate plan to mold the fif-teen into exactly what he needed to kill Swift Raven. He first led them against White men. It took little encouragement. All fifteen hated the wagon trains and homesteads, traders and missionaries, army outposts and military patrols. All things White suffered un-der their savagery. Their fury left no time for anything but killing and burning.

Then pillage and rape were added to their lust. The band had no village or permanent hideout, so material things, unless they could be worn or carried, held no importance. Their long string of attacks introduced them to weapons used only by the White man. The Henry repeating rifle could have further increased the ability of the fifteen to kill quickly and with terrifying efficiency. But the renegades' revulsion for anything having to do with the White man's world resulted in their breaking into pieces any captured gun. If it was White, it must be destroyed. Learning how to use it would be traitorous. Bows and arrows, spears and shields, knives and hatchets were their weapons… Indian weapons!... and they used these with unerring dexterity.

Sky Fire loved the excitement and brutality of their raids. He was their teacher - always in the midst of the most horrendous at-tacks - aiming and shooting, then releasing a second, and a third arrow, one after the other in rapid fire. It might appear that each particular raid was his sole reason for becoming a renegade. But, in truth, he never lost his driving desire to kill the old Indian who had brought about his humiliation. The raids had one ultimate purpose to Sky Fire – they were to hone the abilities of the fifteen to kill without conscience.

If he were to use the renegade band to find Swift Raven, he must switch their vengeance from hating Whites to hating Indians – one Indian in particular. Several tribes were represented among the braves, but they all had common enemies. Satisfied with the demented progress Sky Fire had made with the fifteen thus far, he turned century-old tribal hatreds into reasons for attacking their own race.

The raids on Indian villages were orchestrated, not every-man-for-himself, ruin-and-run. Sky Fire assigned each man to what he could do best and the exact moment he was to do it. Some were to set fire to the tepees, some to drive off the horses, some to kill the men, others to capture the women and girls who would be used and then killed. Sky Fire would not tolerate a single deviation to his plan of attack and each renegade destroyed with complete efficiency. None was seriously hurt, while no enemy was left un-scathed.

Their loot was never greater than scalps and horses. The band of fifteen would ride off with their leader, waving their weapons and emitting victory yells – not because they had laid waste an enemy village, but because their blood lust had been satisfied. Sky Fire was not immune to the exhilaration. His adrenalin coursed as rap-idly as anyone's. But his greatest jubilation would come only after the locating and slaying of Swift Raven.

There were three bucks among the renegades who called them-selves scouts. Sky Fire didn't know how much training or experi-ence they had before leaving the village that might have schooled them in this calling. He put them to tests as he planned various ventures. Sometimes the three succeeded in giving him useful lo-cations, information or warnings. Sometimes they failed and were severely beaten with his quirt.

Finally Sky Fire's complete domination of the band made him confident to begin his personal agenda. One night, Sky Fire called the young renegades around him. "We have shown our superiority over the White men by our raids. We have upheld the pride of our tribes against our enemies, the Witapaha, the Oyatenumpa, the Pani. Now I ask you to follow me to destroy my own enemy." He looked at the three scouts. "Can you track an old Indian traveling with a young boy?"

The bravest of the three asked, "Who are they that we should risk our lives to find and destroy them?"

Sky Fire did not answer but menacingly tapped the handle of his quirt against the side of his leg. All three scouts fell silent. They looked away from the anger burning in his eyes. Sky Fire was leader. He need not explain – only demand. And in truth, after witnessing his vehement nature on many occasions, all three were afraid of him.

The first evidence of the old Indian and the boy was a long-deserted campground where a deer had been butchered. The bones had been picked clean of meat and lay crushed by carnivores' teeth. Any trail used to go further had been overgrown.

The second attempt to locate Swift Raven and Kincade had been stopped by gully-washing rain which inundated even their own tracks. Sky Fire ranted against the three scouts as if they had secretly performed the rain dance and brought on the deluge to spite him.

The third time, Sky Fire took only one scout with him, for wafting smoke from a distance had signaled that only a small fire was burning, needed perhaps by just two people. "Wait here for us," he told the band. "One of you might give warning by the snap of a twig or scrape on a rock or frightened cry of an animal. I shall stand alone as I draw my bow and aim my arrow." Sky Fire howled, "I swear I will kill them both!" The image was so strong in Sky Fire's mind that he crept towards the smoke as though he were in a trance.

Sky Fire readied his arrow as he peered over a low rise. There in a blackened pit were two completely worn out moccasins – one a man's, one a boy's. Smoke slowly smoldered and chewed through the tough leather but the fire had long since gone out.

Sky Fire exploded in anger. He stood, reared back in rage, and spun to hit the scout with his quirt, over and over again. "Couldn't you tell there was no blaze, that they had left long ago? Why have I come all this way only to be made a fool? You are to blame! You call yourself a scout? I call you heyoka, a clown, a contrary who turns everything backwards." He was shouting. "Ride behind me as we return. I do not want the stench of your presence."

* * * * * *

Kincade and Old Indian were preparing for winter. Another deer had been killed and strips of meat were hanging on a rack of aspen branches. The deer skin had been scraped clean and was pegged out on the ground to dry. Berries and nuts had been gathered and stored in pouches of the deer's organs. Swift Raven and Kincade had a day of leisure before starting out again for winter's necessities.

Suddenly the old man stiffened. "Go hide in the woods," he ordered Kincade and the boy obeyed as Swift Raven fitted an arrow into his bow string. From his chosen spot Kincade saw a big horse ridden by a tall Indian who approached with his hands outstretched in friendly greeting. "Kangee Kohana," he called. "The scout Ozuye Najin approaches your camp."

Swift Raven lowered his weapon and rushed forward to greet Standing Warrior, his friend of many years. "How did you find me? I have traveled on secret paths."

"There has only been one scout better than you." He gently touched the old man on the shoulder. "That scout is me. When I need to find you – I find you."

"Before you tell me what that need is, let us smoke a small pipe and remember." Kincade slowly emerged from the aspen grove, assured now that this visitor meant no harm. "Come boy. This is the great scout Ozuye Najin. I have told you stories about him. You may tend to our guest's horse. Lead him to the water and wipe down his coat with soft leaves while my friend and I sit together."

Kincade picked up the jaw-thong and took the horse to water without even trying to listen to the reason for the unexpected visitor.

The two Indians did not jump into conversation but let the sweet smoke curl around their heads in lazy swirls. The only sound was Kincade speaking to the horse. Even the birds were hushed, seeming to await the news that the scout brought to the camp.

The pipe was depleted and laid alongside the cold fire pit. "You have come a long way to find me," Swift Raven began. "Do you come to bring me good news or bad?"

Standing Warrior looked directly at the old man. "Your two daughters, Kimimela Weeko and Ehawee, are now my two wives." He then fell silent.

"I ask again. Is this good news or bad?" There was a slight smile on Swift Raven's lips.

"They persuaded me to find you or else I would not have traveled so far with so much difficulty." The scout also smiled. "Kimimela Weeko divorced Mahpee Paytah and became my second wife because he has vowed to find you and kill you."

"For taking Kincade?"

"Yes. But he also blames you for Kimimela Weeko coming to my tepee as my second wife. His pride will drive him to kill you."

Swift Raven thought on this news for a silent minute. "I take the boy so that the White soldiers will not return him to his White parents. These are the men I should fear, not someone from my own tribe."

"The other White boy, brother to Kincade, was returned to his White father who was the soldier who came for him."

"Will not that same father look again for Kincade?"

"No." Standing Warrior chose not to tell of the soldier's death by the Cougar.

"So, tell me of this Indian who was once my son-in-law and who now I have reason to fear."

"Mahpee Paytah is nothing like the man you once knew. He has become one of the renegade Indians who search and destroy all whom they consider enemies. They have sacked and burned the homes of many White settlers. They attack their Indian enemies with equal terror. Mahpee Paytah is the leader of the group and has ordered them to search for you."

Swift Raven was silent, considering what had been said about Sky Fire. "This is a safe haven. They will not find me."

"I found you - they can find you. You must be on the move again to a more hidden place."

"Do you know of such a place?"

"Only a new place – always - over and over again. Changing each time before the renegade scouts have success."

"And if I choose to stay here?"

"Mahpee Paytah will kill you."

"I am old. That will be a good day to die."

"And what of the boy? Will that be a good day for him to also die? Mahpee Paytah will not return him to his White mother. His hatred of you has now grown to include the boy. Kincade's scalp will hang next to yours from his war shield as a victory trophy."

Swift Raven nodded in understanding. "Will you travel with us and suggest a safer place?"

"No. Even I must not know where you go. Follow the flight of the swift raven which will lead you. His name is your name – Kangee Kohana. That is the message I have to give you. Now I will return to my two wives and tell them to let the Great Spirit make decisions – not them." He stood to go. He signaled to Kincade and the boy brought the horse to his side. The scout mounted with an easy leap and rode away without ever looking back.

Swift Raven looked around at what must be packed away and loaded onto the drags. "We are leaving," he said to Kincade. The boy started to speak. "It is not the Indian Way to ask why. There is much to do." They set to work, loading the drags. All signs of their camp were erased.

To Old Indian it did not seem a miracle that, as they headed out, a raven appeared overhead, flying before them on this, their first day of endless running.

CHAPTER 26

KINCADE CRIED OUT in his sleep. Swift Raven gently touched him behind the ear to awaken him. "Oh it is you, Old Indian! Now I am not afraid."

"Can you tell me your dream?" he asked as the boy sat up blinking.

"Yes, I still remember. There was a boy with a very big knife and he was trying to cut my throat. He slashed back and forth and I kept trying to jump out of his way."

"Are you sure it was a boy and not the man who cut you here?" Swift Raven touched the scars on Kincade's bicep.

"It was a boy about my size. I didn't recognize him. He cut me bad. But then another boy came up and rescued me."

"Was it the Indian boy who saved you from being drowned at the bathing pool?"

"No. That boy is big. This boy was smaller than me but he was very strong. Why did I have such a dream?"

Swift Raven puzzled the tale. "The Spirit Grandfathers send us dreams for understanding, for guidance, for warnings."

"But you explain everything to me that I do not understand. And you are the guide for where we are going. Did the scout Ozuye Najin bring you a warning?"

Swift Raven sighed. The boy was old for his eight years. "This was your dream, not mine. The Spirit Grandfathers set no time for understanding dreams. Sometimes many seasons must pass before the dreamer knows whether his night message was for understanding, guidance, or warning. You must practice The Wait."

"Old Indian, I don't want that dream again." Kincade's young face turned to Swift Raven for help.

"Go to sleep, for this day you will not ride – not on the dog, not with me. Today you will walk."

"Am I being punished?"

"No, you are being taught. You have work to do. You must gather little bird feathers that you will see along the way. And if you see a small green stone, pick it up also. Put these in your loincloth."

"In my loincloth?"

Swift Raven laughed. "You can't carry them all in your hands. Now go to sleep for a little while. I will wake you at first light."

All day Kincade walked unhurriedly, looking to right and left. Swift Raven was not impatient to move any faster. He saw Kincade's slow pace as proof of the care the boy was devoting to the process and opportunity to learn new lessons. He felt great pride.

They stopped earlier than usual and made a simple camp. "Have you found what I asked for?"

Kincade nodded. From his loincloth the boy withdrew five small feathers: red from a cardinal, yellow from a goldfinch, a brown-specked feather from a grouse, a dark blue feather from a jay, and a white feather from a magpie. He also had found three green stones which he laid in Swift Raven's hand.

"You have been very watchful to find all these," he said, smiling at Kincade. "Now I need a branch that will bend easily. Try those bushes over there. Here is my knife but be careful it is only the branch that you cut." Kincade scurried to find one that he thought would be just right. "Perfect. Now go to the edge of the stream and bring me long blades of sweet grass."

When Kincade came back, Swift Raven had curled the branch into a small hoop and secured it by twisting the ends. He took the grass from the boy and carefully wove it back and forth, from side to side, making a green web. "Now I shall hang your feathers around the edge. Hand them to me carefully, one by one." Kincade did. "Now give me the stones." He looked carefully at each and threw away two of them. "This one is true turquoise. You were lucky to find it. I place it in the center and the Dream Catcher will be finished."

Kincade looked with awe at the hoop. "Dream Catcher? You mean it can catch my dreams?"

"We will place it by your head at night. Dreams both good and bad will fall from the sky into this web of sweet grass. This beautiful little piece of turquoise will let all the good dreams pass through the web into your dream. But if any bad dream is caught, the green stone will hold it until daylight returns. Then the warmth of the sun will evaporate the evil and send it back to the sky forever. This is the Indian Way."

Kincade held the hoop with great reverence. "May I go to sleep now and try it out?"

Swift Raven laughed. "I think we should eat something first."

Every night Kincade placed the Dream Catcher by his head and every night it allowed only happy dreams to enter the sleeping boy's mind. A few times he saw the lady with the light skin and brown hair who was singing. But even she faded and before long his dreams of her disappeared entirely. As time passed, Kincade's dreams of his brother Wil ended. In fact, he ceased to think of Wil at all, and gradually he even forgot he once had a different life than traveling constantly with Old Indian.

There was no forgetting Kincade in Agnes's house where Wil and his mother now lived.

"Wil, why won't you carry in the wood and draw the water? Kincade was always so helpful."

Wil looked at her defiantly.

"Why are you so stupid?" said Angela. "Kincade learned that when he was only four!" She shook her head in dismay. "Your teacher came by to say you can't attend class any more. You stole some poor child's lunch bucket and then beat him up when he tried to get it back! Kincade would never have done something so mean!

"Mr. Winnaby says you were smoking in his barn and set the hay on fire! He wants me to pay for the damage! Kincade never would have done that! Why can't you be good like him?"

Wil shouted back. "Like he was, you mean! He's dead and gone! The bears et him and I'm glad – else I would'a et him myself!"

Angela went into her room, sobbing. "If they had to find only one of my sons, why did it have to be Wil!"

CHAPTER 27

SWIFT RAVEN HAD been watching the dusty horizon for several hours. As last he slid from the horse and handed Kincade the jaw-thong. He knelt on his boney knees and put his ear to the ground. Then he stood and helped Kincade off the horse. "We will stay here."

"Forever and ever, Old Indian?"

"Only the Great Spirit knows. Help me unload the drags. We will set up the tepee near the stream."

That was truly good news for Kincade could again climb the securing pins and scoop out the central fire pit. He would hang the Dream Catcher over his side of the buffalo robe. He was learning not to wonder how long anything was to last. Just like Swift Raven said, it was not the Indian Way. He must practice The Wait.

But he was sometimes curious. "Did the ground tell you that we should stay here?"

"Not the ground, but what rumbles over the ground. Pte."

"Buffalo?" Swift Raven nodded as he unfolded the tepee cover. "Why would we stop for buffalo?"

"Because I shall kill one and we will have much meat and another robe for winter."

Kincade was ten years old and he had never seen a live buffalo up close, but he had seen them from a distance. They had huge shaggy heads with sharp horns. He knew how mighty the creatures were for their big skins made the cover of the tepee and a warm hide made the bed they slept on. Old Indian had told him buffalos were the lords of the prairie upon whom the very existence of a tribe depended. Only the bravest Indians went to kill them on their most skilled horses. The boy looked at the little, wrinkled, scrawny old man. Old Indian was going to kill one of these awesome beasts? How? He looked at the drag horse. It could not chase a slow rabbit let alone a charging buffalo. These things Kincade pondered but he knew that his questions could only be answered by watching and practicing The Wait. So he unloaded the drags, took the two animals to water, and helped raise the tepee. Then he waited for Swift Raven to go kill a buffalo.

At last Swift Raven said, "Bring the horse with the drag." He was carrying his bow and a quiver of arrows.

"Shall I bring my weapon?"

Swift Raven smiled. "I may need all the help I can get." He motioned to walk quietly toward a knoll about a half mile away. At the crest they lay on their stomachs and looked down on a small herd of about a hundred buffalo. They had kept downwind of the beasts which had no hint of their presence.

"Take off your clothes," Swift Raven whispered as he stripped down to his loincloth and moccasins. "You are easier to clean than they are." He twisted back his long hair into a knot and secured his skinning knife to a sheath on his leg.

"You remember what you are to do?"

"Yes, thank one of them for giving up its life for us. Which one?"

"That one!" Swift Raven pointed as he dashed down the gentle slope with the speed of a youth. Exhilarated by memories of his hunting days he shouted, "i-i-ya! i-i-ya! i-i-ya!" Like a signal gun had been fired, heads went up, tails lifted and curled, and a bellow of confusion rippled over the alerted mass which began to run. A fat cow had been lying down and she was making an effort to get to her feet and join the herd. As Swift Raven came alongside he pulled his knife from its leg sheath and slashed at her hind legs. She fell to her forelegs and instantly Swift Raven's arrow found its mark in her lungs. There was a mournful bellow. Then a second arrow pierced her kidneys. A mighty convulsing, a tail flailing the air, and then stillness. The rest of the herd had become a rumble of fleeing hooves in the distance.

From the knoll Kincade had watched with his heart in his mouth. "What if the buffalo kills Old Indian? Where would I go? What would I do?" His small bow and arrows were no comfort. Now that the killing was over and the only one dead was a buffalo, he let out his own "i-i-ya! i-i-ya! i-i-ya!" as he led the pack horse down the slope.

Swift Raven began skinning away the tough hide. When Kincade arrived he cut out the liver and lifted the still warm body part to his few teeth, taking a large bite. He held it out to Kincade. "This will give us strength to finish what must be done here." So Kincade sunk his teeth into the liver, feeling for the first time that he was a grown up Indian.

Swift Raven smiled and handed the boy his big knife. "Have you learned enough to do the rest of the job?"

"I shall try. Where do I start?"

Swift Raven showed him how to cut away the hump and tongue - the choicest portions which they would roast or boil. They also harvested the less tasty, but equally nourishing, meat for jerky and pemmican. The brains, slabs of fat, and large bones which held marrow were taken for tanning purposes. They loaded all these into the pte skin, and heaved it onto the drag. Last of all, Swift Raven cut off the tail of the buffalo and tossed it onto the heap.

"Are we going to eat that too?" Kincade looked at the ropelike tail.

"No. You are going to swish it." Once again Kincade knew he would have to practice The Wait for understanding.

Swift Raven looked with regret at all that was left on the ground. Then slowly he sank to his knees, closed his eyes and threw back his head. From deep within his soul he made the call of a wolf, so real that Kincade could not believe that an actual animal had not howled.

"Old Indian, are you talking to the wolves?" he asked timidly.

Swift Raven did not answer but once again threw back his head and made an even longer howl. From far away there was an answering call. At first Kincade thought it was an echo, but it sounded again and Swift Raven had been silent. Soon he opened his eyes and looked at the boy.

"We are unable to use more of this noble creature, so I have invited our brothers, the wolves, to a feast. Since you promised the buffalo that nothing would be wasted, I have made guests of the creatures most deserving our good fortune. Come, we must not keep them waiting too long."

With that, Swift Raven took the jaw-thong and led the horse back up the slope while Kincade followed, his eyes constantly looking back and forth.

Soon, the wolves would come.

CHAPTER 28

THE SUN WAS setting by the time they got back to the tepee. They plunged into the stream to soak the blood from their weary bodies. But Swift Raven would not let them stay long and soon they were unloading the drag and starting to work. The hide was spread out in the stream to be washed and rewashed all night long until the dirt and salt were removed and the skin softened. Kincade was told to put the meat harvest in paunches and suspend them high, out of reach of night-prowling animals. Swift Raven laughed when Kincade's height proved too short to swing the cargo to safety, so the old man gingerly climbed a tree and did it himself.

"We have earned a good dinner," he decided. "Find some green branches and we will hang slices of the tongue over the fire to roast. Tomorrow we will be even busier than today."

The buffalo hide was heavy when wet but they managed to drag it to an open space and spread it, fur side down. Swift Raven fashioned sharp wooden stakes from tree branches and pegged the hide to the ground to be stretched and tanned. Kincade was put to work with a stone scrapper, cleaning away the adhering bits of tissue and membranc. The dog yelped gleefully as the boy tossed him bits which were snapped down without even tasting.

Swift Raven didn't trust Kincade's skill with the big skinning knife, so he sliced all the less succulent meat into thin, narrow strips. "We shall make jerky with half. Help me hang it near the fire to catch the smoke." Kincade did. "Now help me hang the rest on bushes in the bright sunlight to cure for pemmican."

A flock of magpies had discovered the butchery and besides his other duties Kincade was kept busy flailing with the buffalo tail to drive them away. All during his frantic activity a black raven had hopped around the campsite, squawking and begging for food. Swift Raven told Kincade not to drive this bird away, and he tossed tidbits and laughed when the raven flew to a tree branch to eat.

"Old Indian, I want to know why you feed the raven when you try to keep other birds from attacking our meat?"

"He will show me his gratitude whenever it is time," was all that Swift Raven would say.

While the hide was still damp, Swift Raven mixed together the brains, marrow and melted fat, spreading it from the center to the edge. "Take off your moccasins. We will have some fun." Slipping and sliding over the skin, they worked the goo into the pores until the tough hide was soft and pliable. After rinsing it off, they pulled and stretched it again and again, resetting the stakes, until it reached its maximum size. Then they left it to dry.

Every meal they feasted on meat which would spoil if not eaten within days. Swift Raven kept feeling the thin strips that had been drying on the bushes and one day he finally said, "They are now ready to be pounded into a powder. We will also pound all our remaining dried berries and mix them together with melted fat. This pemmican will see us through the winter."

The day came when the raven did not caw for food but flew back and forth from ground to tree top, disappearing into the sky and then swooping back to earth again. Swift Raven watched. "I understand," he called after the messenger. "Come, Kincade. We must pack up and move."

"I heard you call to the wolves. Do you also understand the raven?"

The old man looked Kincade in the eyes, hoping the young boy could understand. "From time to time everyone lives with uncertainty, asking, should I? – should I not? You are never at peace in this situation. When you are shown the truth, ask no more questions – act. It is the Indian Way."

As the pack animals pulled the drag poles away from the campsite, Kincade walked behind brushing the ground with a stiff branch, scattering debris and erasing all signs of which direction they had taken to depart.

*   *   *   *   *

The next time Sky Fire ordered a trek to search for the old Indian and child, all three scouts huddled together. They tossed the marked berry stones from the little wooden bowl to see who would go with their leader this time. As luck would have it, the same scout who had found only burning moccasins lost the final throw. He mounted his horse and gave the others one last look as he followed Sky Fire out of the encampment.

Sky Fire stormed around the deserted campsite, kicking at buffalo bones and ashes in a dead fire pit. He shook his spear at the scout. "This is the fourth time you have told me you could find the old Indian who deserves to die. And each time he has outsmarted you and left long before we can arrive. A lazy camp-dog would make a better tracker."

The scout knew better than to offer excuses to this leader of the band of renegades. He had been accused and insulted by Sky Fire several times before. He knew how dangerous Sky Fire was. He turned his horse to ride out of the abandoned camp.

"Stop!" Sky Fire shouted. "A leader should not have to follow such stupidity – not ever – and not one more time. You have led your last failure." With lightning speed, he threw his spear with the deadly accuracy by which he had become known, the obsidian head ripping through the neck of the scout. The man died instantly, falling to the ground without uttering a single cry.

Sky Fire mounted his black horse and rode back and forth over the crumpled body, crushing bone, splitting the scout's skull like a ripe squash. He screamed at the sky, "I came here to kill!" Sky Fire yanked the spear from what was left of the eviscerated body beneath the horse's hooves. Looking at the human gore, Sky Fire snarled, "You were not my first choice to kill. But not a bad choice, because I will never have to trust you again!"

Sky Fire spun his horse around, leaving nothing but the scout's body behind.

Leaving nothing, except for one raven who watched Sky Fire from a tree branch high above… watched with unblinking black eyes.

CHAPTER 29

WHEN SKY FIRE returned alone from this fourth attempt to find Swift Raven, he gave no explanation as to the disappearance of the scout who had gone with him, and no one dared to ask. The two remaining scouts looked at one another. Had the toss of the big seeds chosen their brother for death? Did the two of them dare play the game ever again? Neither of them wanted to be chosen as the next scout to lead Sky Fire on his relentless pursuit. During that night both disappeared into the darkness.

They were not the only ones deserting the fanatical leader. Men who had once joined in the raids with unabashed enthusiasm began sneaking away. For some, they had sewn their wild oats and now longed to marry. It was the custom for a man to live with his wife's tribe, and brother renegades had offered their sisters as suitable women for any who wished to return to village life. It was even suggested, although not within Sky Fire's hearing, that they should set up their own village and bring captured women to become wives for those staying.

For others, it was no longer enough to go on raids for the thrill and challenge. The men wanted to acquire wealth, but where were they to bring it if they were outcasts? Some wanted power, but how could they acquire leadership when Sky Fire tolerated no contender for his position?

All these reasons contributed to the ever-diminishing size of the renegade band. But no motivation to leave was stronger than Sky Fire's obsession with finding an old Indian and a boy. Pursuing his personal vendetta did not inspire their loyalty and discipline as had the early years of raiding and destroying.

By the sixth year, Sky Fire had only three followers. These men were the worst of the lot, true savages that lived only for the blood thirst of killing. They had not made the decision to leave their villages to become renegades. They had been driven out of their societies because they showed neither restraint nor clear judgment. They had no honor and that suited Sky Fire perfectly.

Sky Fire's leadership had honed them into perfect weapons. All three had proved themselves to be heartless and cruel without a shred of conscience. Their killing was never without torture; their raping was never without brutality; their destruction was never without total obliteration. At times Sky Fire believed their fanaticism was even greater than his own. It was this thought that started him carefully watching for treachery against himself. They were certainly capable of it.

Sky Fire followed their eyes whenever the four sat silently around the fire. He sensed their exchange of secret plans. Stealthily he listened to their whispered conversations which would abruptly stop when his presence was realized. Sky Fire became certain that his position as leader – in fact, his very life - was threatened by the three remaining renegades. He wasn't surprised. He had trained them to be killers. Why would their training exclude killing the one who had trained them?

Sky Fire would act before they could. He plotted to put them out of his way. He told them their next raid would be on a trading post which they had not sacked for several years.

After the usual destruction and debauchery they rode away. This time, Sky Fire's plunder included two jugs of the White man's whiskey. Previously the leader had never allowed the renegades to steal fire water for he knew its addictive power could destroy as easily as delight. But after this raid, Sky Fire paid hollow tribute to the three renegades, hoisting the jugs on high. He shouted "Your new triumph should be rewarded with new pleasure!"

That night as the four sat around a fire, Sky Fire passed the jugs. The three slurped down the burning liquid. Never had they experienced such a taste. Their leader only put the jug to his lips, pretending to swallow as the intoxication of the others increased.

By midnight the three were sprawled out like staked buffalo skins, their heavy breathing only broken by slobber from blubbering lips.

Sky Fire walked slowly around his adversaries with a smile on his face. As the coals of the fire cast deep shadows across the sleeping bodies, Sky Fire raised his hatchet and with two deft slashes at the throat he decapitated the first renegade. The eyes popped open but not a peep was heard from the severed head. On to the next, with the same quiet dispatch. Then the third. Their eyes were all open; their tongues hung out as if the heads desired to say some final word.

Sky Fire raised a war cry into the dark night. He picked up his spear and jammed the sharp point into all six eyes, laughing as one by one they stopped their staring. "Never again will you look at me with envious plotting." He pulled out their tongues and sliced them from their throats. "Never again will you mumble accusation and insults against me." Their necks were rising above pools of blood but their bodies were twitching with a last effort for life. Sky Fire whacked them into little pieces. "The better for the vultures to feast upon." He laughed maniacally.

Sky Fire's exhilarated butchery of the three surpassed every other experience of his life. He was now free of stupidity, of treachery, of insubordination. He became enthralled in his own egotism. He felt newly alive with his fresh determination to find and kill Swift Raven.

This supreme adoration of himself must be celebrated with another new experience. He picked up the whiskey jug. He put it to his nose to savor the inviting aroma. He swished the liquid around. "The jug is almost half full," he said. "No one is left to threaten me. I pay tribute to me - to ME!"

Sky Fire raised the jug to his mouth and ran his tongue around its neck. The taste was beyond temptation, it was a demand. He tipped the jug and drank until the final drops spilled from his lips. Then he waved it to the moon cresting over the campsite. "I am Mahpee Paytah!" he shouted. "Nothing like me ever was or will ever be again!"

The fire of the White man's liquor consumed him. Within moments, the whiskey took full effect, rushing through the walls of his stomach directly into the blood stream. He fell to the ground and into the sticky pools of blood flowing from the men he had just murdered.

CHAPTER 30

IT SEEMED TO Kincade that the first priority of every season was to prepare to face the following one. All during the warm months Swift Raven and Kincade hunted the larger animals so that their skins could be tanned and ready for winter sewing. Much of the meat was dried or smoked. Edible roots were dug up and put in paunches. Berries were picked and dried and nuts harvested. Summer was a time of looking ahead, but also a time of pleasure.

They traveled more in the summer, moving when the raven told the old man to change sites. The bird remained with them always. Kincade wasn't sure if it was because Old Indian threw it scraps of meat, or because it really was a guarding spirit that led them onward. He didn't dwell on speculation for Old Indian would say, "Watch and listen and someday you will know."

As Swift Raven and Kincade walked to hunt or gather, they played a learning game. "What does the sky tell you?" the old man asked.

"It speaks to me of the weather living in the clouds. There will be rain, or lightning, or the little ice balls. It tells me that the birds circling overhead see something dead on the ground. It shows me that I may be able to find water where many yellow butterflies are hovering low over the land."

"Ah, very good." They walked further. "Now look at this ground. What does it tell you?"

"It tells me these tracks were made by the wolf and not the coyote." And further on, "This is a deer's hoof print, not an antelope's."

"Ah, very good. You have used your eyes up and down." Swift Raven was walking behind Kincade. "STOP! NOW! Where you are standing! Use your ears!"

Kincade was very still, and then he heard what Swift Raven had heard. "The snake with the rattling tail is close by."

"Are you afraid of that snake?"

"No, Old Indian. He sees with eyes that never close but he only sees that which moves. If I am very still he will not see me."

"I will kill it with a big rock and we will have it for dinner." Swift Raven's action was too fast for the snake to detect and he picked up the slimy creature that lay dead in the grass. "He will not always warn you, Kincade. Never put your hands or your feet where you cannot see. It is the Indian Way."

They walked on. "I have another question for you to answer," Swift Raven said. He touched the tip of his nose. "What do I smell?"

Kincade sniffed the air. "You smell an herb - sage. Am I right?"

"Yes, so find it and let us return to make our supper of excellent snake meat soup."

When the cold moon signaled winter's approach, Swift Raven headed for the hills where caves or stands of close timber could give them shelter. A supply of water was always a consideration, either a small stream which could be chipped free of ice or a spring in the back of a cave. Once the site had been chosen they gathered many fallen branches and piled them close by to keep a warm fire constantly going. The horse and dog would need shelter as well, and Swift Raven constructed a thicket barrier against blowing snow.

During the cold months they planned for the warmth to return. Each season Kincade grew taller and needed longer leggings and shirts and bigger moccasins. Swift Raven insisted he make his own. So Kincade learned to sew with a bone awl and carefully harvested tendons. "Old Indian, must I also learn to quill?"

"No, that is women's work." And they both laughed for many things they did were traditionally the work of women.

"You are growing into a man," Swift Raven said as he held up a new garment. "It is time you had a man's bow, not the childish thing that kills only rabbits and gophers. I have already found a good piece of iron wood, but you must help me fashion it."

And so one winter Kincade learned to draw a stout bow and let fly arrows with speed and precision. When the weather was good and the wild animals crept from their dens to find food, they would hunt for fresh meat to supplement the jerky and pemmican. Swift Raven also made Kincade a spear. He taught the boy to throw it with accuracy by sending a loop along a path and Kincade was to hit the center as it rolled by.

The best thing about winter was the story telling which had delighted Kincade as a boy. Swift Raven seemed to have an endless supply of tales, but even if he repeated Kincade's favorites he gave them a different twist. It was now Kincade's turn to act out the characters as Swift Raven related their antics. The hero was usually an animal - a turkey, a turtle, a duck or a coyote. As Kincade mimicked their actions and sometimes their voices, both of them would fall over laughing. But Swift Raven always reminded him, "This earth is a gift of the Great Spirit and all creatures only travel through it. Mankind is not more important to Wakan Tanka than any other creation – animal, bird, reptile, tree, or stone. We are all brothers and can speak to one another if only we listen."

"Is that why you can talk to the raven who is hopping around us at this very moment?"

"I do not talk to him for I am earthbound and I know nothing that he needs to hear. He talks to me because he looks down from his winged flight and sees what I need to know. We are brothers."

"I would like to have a brother – but one that I can understand."

Swift Raven thought, "You do have a brother, but you will never understand him."

During the winter that Kincade was twelve, the dog died. There was no grieving for it had never been a pet, only a beast of burden. When the spring thaws came and the black bird told Swift Raven to get ready to travel again, the man said to the boy, "It is time you have your own horse. You are too big now to ride with me and we need an animal for the second drag. Yes, you need your own horse."

This was thrilling news to the boy. He had felt for some time that he had outgrown the childish way of riding double. "How do I get a horse, Old Indian?"

"There are two ways. We could try to find a herd of wild horses and capture one of them for you to train for riding. That would be more difficult and take longer."

"What is the easier, faster way? If we are about to travel again we don't have much time." He wanted his own horse as soon as possible.

"The second way is to steal one."

Kincade thought this over very carefully. He could not remember ever seeing another person, except the scout Standing Warrior and Old Indian would not steal his horse if he ever returned. "I don't understand how that is possible," he finally said.

"Follow me."

They left the tepee and their belongings behind and both rode on Swift Raven's horse for most of the afternoon. When they approached a valley below the plains they had been crossing, Swift Raven motioned that they should get off and go on foot. At the crest of a butte they lay on their stomachs and peered below. There was a village of at least fifty tepees, erected in a large circle. People and animals were moving, although they seemed far away.

Kincade stared in disbelief. The scene was strangely familiar. It almost frightened him as if he were looking into some secret realm of stories. "What is it, Old Indian?" he asked.

"It is an Indian village."

Kincade tried to remember. "Did we used to live in one?"

"Yes."

"Why did we leave?"

Swift Raven knew that one day this question would be asked, but he hadn't decided yet what he would answer. He stared at the scene for a long time and Kincade knew not to ask again. Finally he said, "I steal something that I want very bad from a powerful brave. I cannot go back unless I return it. I am not ready."

Kincade thought but did not say, "He's probably lost it by now and is too proud to admit it." But he asked, "Was it a horse?"

Swift Raven looked at the boy with as much affection as was ever seen in his sagging eyes. "No, it was not a horse."

"But you plan to steal a horse now from that village down there?"

"Yes."

"Will they come after you with bows and arrows?" Kincade did not want to be left alone so far from their camp.

"I will do it after it gets dark and all are asleep. Prepare yourself to mount and ride swiftly when I bring a horse back."

Kincade lay on his stomach and watched the people below. Some were wearing long shirts and were doing things around the camp that he had to do. Others only wore leggings like himself and Old Indian and appeared to do very little. He thought of the creatures of the forest. There were two sexes. "The ones in the long shirts - are they the females?"

"Yes. They are called women. Do you remember knowing women?"

"I have dreamed of two persons wearing long shirts and doing work like those women below us. But then these two persons become you and me." Old Indian could not hold back his laughter and Kincade wondered what was so funny.

"Have you known women, Old Indian?"

"I have known many women but only one I want to remember."

Kincade watched them walking gracefully and talking with one another. "Old Indian, do you understand women?"

"There are two ways to understand women. We shall discuss them as we wait for darkness to overtake the village."

They slid back down from the butte and led the horse where it wouldn't be seen. "Did you say two ways?" Kincade wanted to get back to the subject they had never mentioned before.

"Yes, but neither one of them works." Swift Raven laughed and passed Kincade jerky to chew during their fascinating discussion.

It was very dark when Swift Raven returned leading a horse. Kincade mounted without being able to see the beast. As he held the jaw-thong and nudged its ribs he realized that it was gentle and responsive.

Swift Raven said, "The star that never changes its place in the sky will guide us back." They galloped through the darkness and Kincade was thankful they were not followed.

The remainder of the night Kincade lay awake wondering what his very own horse looked like. At first light he was up. The horse was where Swift Raven had hobbled it near grass and water. Kincade thought it was the most wonderful horse he had ever seen. Never mind that its color was a dull brown or that its head and ears were small. Never mind that its tail had been cropped and its mane needed combing. Kincade's ownership gave the animal an unsurpassed beauty. He put his arms around its neck and pressed the damp nose to his cheek. "I shall call you Thunder.. ...if that is okay with Old Indian for he is the one who stole you."

"Thunder is a good name." Swift Raven was sitting up from his sleeping robe. "Will you now fix some food. Then we will load the drags, for the raven is telling me that today is a good day to travel."

The tepee was dismantled and the drag poles laid in position to load, when Swift Raven stopped in his tracks. He hurried to get his bow and quiver of arrows. A horse and rider were approaching at a slow pace. "Get your weapon and stand ready," he told Kincade. "Perhaps I am not as clever a thief as I thought."

The rider approached leading a handsome appaloosa horse that had a raven sitting on its rump. "Kangee Kohana," he called. "I am still better at tracking than you ever were."

Swift Raven put down his weapon and rushed forward to greet Standing Warrior. "You can say, 'as good as', but not 'better'. I am surprised to see you for I left no clue for you to find us."

"I always find you - from time to time." The raven flew to a nearby branch to watch and listen.

"Oh? You have sneaked up on us before? But you do not ever come to speak with me?"

"I sometimes find you only to report to my two wives that their father has not yet been found by one who threatens to kill him." He then saw Kincade currying his new horse. Standing Warrior dismounted and whispered, "I want to thank you for stealing one of Kimimela Weeko's pack horses and not my own buffalo runner. Had you led him away I would need to kill you even after all our many years of friendship." They both chuckled. "I have news that will be of interest to you."

"And I shall be eager to hear it. But first let us smoke a short pipe and talk of pleasant things. There are still coals in the fire. Kincade, bring more wood and then join us in a smoke." Kincade had never smoked before but he had been told the significance of the pipe. The bowl and stem are the pathway to the heart, and the smoke becomes a sacred truth. He hurried to gather wood chips and join the grown men seated at the fire pit.

"How are my two daughters, Kimimela Weeko and Ehawee?" Swift Raven puffed and passed the pipe to Standing Warrior.

"My wives are well. Kimimela Weeko has presented me with two fine sons since last you and I smoked." Standing Warrior inhaled deeply and passed the pipe to Kincade who pressed the stem to his lips but did not inhale. "Ehawee's oldest boy is now big enough for his own horse."

Kincade interrupted. "I now have my own horse." Then he turned crimson for perhaps he should not have said anything. He quickly handed the pipe to Swift Raven.

Standing Warrior smiled. "One of my reasons for following you is to bring the appaloosa to the father of my two wives – as a gift from them." He took the pipe and puffed silently for a moment.

Swift Raven's look inspected the black horse with white spots on its rump. It was a superb animal. "Thank my daughters. It is a generous gift." The smoke curled.

"Ehawee's best pack horse has suddenly disappeared and she is brokenhearted," the scout said.

"Interesting that a good pack animal happened to wander into our camp this morning. I shall make her a gift of it in return for the appaloosa. Kincade, will you please take the hobbles off Thunder? I think that Lightning has just struck our camp."

Kincade hopped to his feet. He wondered, Lightning? Has Old Indian named the appaloosa Lightning? Will it be mine? He knew, as always, to practice The Wait for the answers would come. He unhobbled the stolen horse and led it back to the fire pit. Swift Raven motioned that Kincade should busy himself elsewhere.

The two men, now sitting alone, puffed without need for words. But when the pipe was empty, Standing Warrior broke the silence. "I bring news of the one who wishes to kill you."

"You mean Mahpee Paytah?"

"Is there another? Acquiring news of more than one might prove difficult." They both smiled.

"Does he still search for the two of us?"

"I sometimes wonder if he remembers who he is searching for. He travels alone now for he became disliked and distrusted by those who once called him their leader. He now drinks the firewater that the White men make. When he drinks it he acts crazy, killing only small boys and old men. His brutality is becoming so fearful that when our people know he is in their area, old men and small boys are sent away into hiding. The White people have no such knowledge and those who cross the plains in rolling wagons or dwell in dirt houses have lost grandfathers and sons while women and daughters remain untouched."

"That is strange. It tells me that his river of life has a whirlpool where the past is trapped and goes round and round, unable to escape."

"Now he prefers a gun to bows and arrows. The gun has a long reach. He can be very far away and yet hit his mark."

"You think that now I can be an easy mark?"

"Unless you are even more cautious. I do not want to ever bring sad news back to my two wives."

"Nor do I want them to receive any." Swift Raven stood and went to the appaloosa. "My old horse and I are too familiar with one another. If it will not offend my two daughters, Kincade can ride this gift horse and care for it as if it were his own."

"That will please Kimimela Weeko. She says her first child was the boy brought to her by Mahpee Paytah."

"What do you call the first child she has given you?"

"Since he is a replacement for the son you stole from her, she named him Kincade, but we call him Kin-Kin."

"And what do you call the second son?"

"We call him Kan-Kan."

"This is his short name?" Standing Warrior nodded. "What is his long name?"

"I regret to have to tell you. When he was making his entrance into this world, a large black raven flew around and around the tepee. So we named him Kangee Kohana."

Swift Raven laughed so hard to hear that the baby had been given his name that he had to hold his belly with both hands.

CHAPTER 31

TWELVE YEAR OLD Wil Logan was the youngest of the four hooligans who sat behind the livery, smoking big cigars they had stolen from the General Store. "You wanna see my mama's titties?" He blew a smoke ring, waiting for their astonishment.

"Hell, yes!" all three answered. "How you gonna do that?"

"Just follow me."

They crept down side streets until they came to Agnes's house with the white picket fence. Wil put his finger to his lips signaling for them to be quiet as he opened the gate and they squatted against the fence posts. Angela was sitting in the rocker on the porch, softly humming, "….poor lonesome Mother. Mother said to God; please send me a little boy; the sweetest one you have in heaven." She rocked a small pillow back and forth in her arms.

Wil whispered, "She thinks that pillow is my twin brother. Just wait a minute, she's gonna feed him."

Angela finished the song. "Is my sweet Kincade a hungry boy? There, there, don't cry. Mama loves you." She unbuttoned her blouse all the way and held the pillow to her naked breast, rocking back and forth.

"Holy geehosefat!" one of the boys said. They all stared wide-eyed.

"Does this every day about this time," Wil told them. "She's crazy."

Angela changed the pillow to her other breast and sat rocking and singing, "God sent Mother her own Kincade; eensie, weensie, tiny, little..."

Agnes stormed through the gate. "You wicked, wicked boys!" She grabbed Wil by the ear and threw him into the street. "Son of the devil! Get away – all of you." She marched up to the porch. "Angela, cover yourself!"

"But Kincade isn't through nursing."

"Then finish up in the house." She pulled her sister from the chair and shoved her through the door.

"Careful, you'll wake him up."

Agnes grabbed the pillow and threw it into a chair. "What am I ever going to do with you?"

Angela smiled in her sweet, wistful way. "You do love Kincade and me, don't you, dearest?"

Agnes embraced Angela, feeling bad about her impatience with her deranged sister. Lord knew it wasn't Angela's fault, given all that had happened to her at the hands of Archibald Logan. "Of course I do." But she muttered under her breath, "It's Wil that I hate... Archie's devil son."

It was impossible for Agnes to leave Angela alone while she went to assist women expecting a child or in the throws of labor. Her sister wandered the streets, calling for Kincade to stop playing hide and seek and come to Mother. Sometimes Wil deliberately led her on by keeping just a few buildings ahead of her and calling, "Here I am, Mama. Bet you can't find me. Come and catch Kincade, Mama." Then he would dash on and she would be searching and calling, much to the shame or amusement of the townspeople.

Agnes came to the realization that she could no longer be a midwife. She would have to find some way to keep body and soul together at home where she could keep an eye on her mad sister. She carefully printed several little cards: "Agnes Johnson will do washing, ironing, and sewing in her home for a reasonable price. To arrange for service, please come to her house on Walnut Street or contact Mr. Emerson at the General Store." It was with great embarrassment that she asked at the post office, the church, and several stores if she might post these on their information boards.

The response was not encouraging. It was a bitter realization that the good life she had lived as a midwife was a thing of the past. But she loved her sister beyond words, and felt such pity that even poverty was worth her sacrifice. She carefully hid the few coins she earned in a broken cookie jar in the back of a kitchen cupboard. She and Angela would survive – if only barely.

The one-story house was not large. There was only an all purpose room with kitchen in a corner and one bedroom. Agnes and Angela slept in the same bed. The attic had enough headroom for Wil to sleep there on an old mattress when he wanted to show up – which wasn't often. He sometimes raided the food in the house but never came to meals. He usually stole from the café or General Store enough to satisfy his hunger. Agnes was always relieved when a day went by without someone complaining or accusing Wil of mischief or outright crime. Angela didn't even realize this son existed, let alone assume any responsibility for his behavior. Agnes endured because she didn't know how to make a change…. short of dying.

"Angela!" Her voice sounded frantic. Her precious money was

gone! "Have you found the cookie jar in the cupboard?"

"No, but maybe Kincade knows where it is. I will ask him." She called, "Kincade, darling..."

But Agnes did not wait. Wil had slept in the house the night before. She knew what had happened to her money. She stormed out of the house without a thought as to leaving Angela alone. "That dirty, thieving, no-good..," she kept repeating as she combed the streets. "When I find him, I'll beat him good." She finally found him behind the livery smoking big cigars with his three friends.

Agnes yanked Wil to his feet. "Where is my money?!" She pulled the cigar from between his teeth and ground it under her heel.

"Don't know what you're talking about. I don't have your money, Auntie Agnes." He could hardly keep from laughing.

"Cause you spent it on those foul smelling cigars?" With a strong thrust that only her anger could inflict, she threw Wil to the ground and emptied out his pockets. There was a little under fourteen dollars in small change which she jammed in her pocket.

"You are a heartless thief, Wil Logan! I want you out of my house!"

"I ain't in your house, Auntie Agnes!" Wil got to his feet and smirked at his friends.

"Don't you 'Auntie' me. I'm through with you! I'm throwing everything of yours into the street. You can't live in my house any more!" She turned and stormed away.

"Bye, bye, Auntie Agnes."

One of the other boys gave him a puff on his cigar. "Crusty old bitty, ain't she. You're just as well off without her."

"You got that right!" The four strutted off to find what else they could do for fun.

Agnes awoke in the middle of the night. Startled, she discovered she was alone in the bed. "Angela," she called. There was no answer. It was bitterly cold in the house for there wasn't enough money to buy coal. She got out of bed and put a shawl around her shoulders. "Angela," she called as she walked through the house, but she could see from wall to wall and knew that her sister was not there. In a panic she opened the front door. A steady cold rain was falling, turning the night blackness into a curtain of gloom. "My God! Where can she be?"

Agnes went back inside and pulled on her old winter coat and heavy boots. She lit a lantern in the kitchen and with great trepidation started to search for her sister on the streets of town.

An hour later she found Angela, huddled in the doorway of the church. Her nightgown was soaked through and through, clinging to her thin shivering body. She was crying.

"Oh, Agnes, I'm so glad you're here. I can't find Kincade anywhere and he must come in out of this terrible rain or he'll catch his death of cold. Have you seen him?"

"Yes, dearest. He is at home. Come let me help you up and we will go to him and all have a cup of hot tea." Her heart was breaking as she pulled her shabby coat around both of them.

The drizzle turned to snow before they reached the house. Angela was barefoot. "I'm so cold, Agnes. Can you carry me?"

"I will try if you'll put your arm around my shoulder." So they limped back to the cold house.

Agnes took off Angela's sodden clothes and dried her hair and shaking body as best she could with a thin towel. "Where is Kincade? I must tuck him in bed."

"He is already asleep. Now put on my dry gown and I'll tuck you in too. I'll get you warm by cuddling close."

"Goodnight, dear Agnes. You are so very, very good to me and Kincade."

"Goodnight, sweet little sister." She could not hold back her sobs, but Angela fell asleep without even noticing.

Next day Angela was coughing and running a fever. Agnes did all she had learned as a midwife to bring the high temperature down and sooth her rasping throat. There was no money to call the doctor, but when Angela got worse and worse still, Agnes went to ask the old physician if she could do some washing and ironing in exchange for his service. The doctor came and after listening to Angela's chest he took Agnes aside. "She is in a very bad way. Had I come sooner, maybe...."

Agnes burst into tears. It was too much to bear. "Is there anything I can do?"

"Try to keep her warm and give her liquids. The rest is in God's hands. I am sorry."

He left and Agnes crumpled onto the floor and prayed. "Dear God, give me strength, and forgive me if I wish these days to be over soon."

In less than a week Angela died. Agnes went to the mortician and exchanged her domestic services for a simple pine box. She then went to the church and begged the pastor to perform a simple ceremony and bury Angela in the Christian graveyard. She would wash and iron for his wife for a month. There was nothing more she could do except dress the body in her own best frock and place a kiss on the white forehead of the only person she had ever loved.

The funeral service was a short, dismal affair. There were only two people seated in the pews – Agnes and a soldier in his dress uniform. Her eyes were so full of tears that she hardly looked at him, but as she stood to go he stopped her.

"Excuse me, Miss Johnson. I hope you will forgive me for intruding, but I knew Mrs. Logan when she lived on the prairie. I used to bring her groceries."

Agnes dried her eyes. "Oh yes. Your name is Harry. Am I right?"

"Yes, Miss. Harry Cogswell. I'm stationed in town now and I've known about your sister's….." He hesitated. "….problems. She was a lovely lady and I liked her a lot. I'm sorry about…."

"Thank you for coming, Harry. She liked you too." Agnes rushed out the door, unable to say more.

As Harry left the church he saw a ragged boy standing near the graveyard fence. He looked remotely familiar and Harry approached him. "Are you Wil Logan?"

"What's it to ya' if I am?" The boy had been crying and wiped his eyes.

"I'm Harry from the Fort. Do you remember me?"

"So what if I do?"

"I've heard unpleasant things about you, Wil. But your mother was very dear to me and I'll not have her son go without food and shelter. If you are hungry or cold you can come to my rooms behind the Army Office. Good day to you." Harry turned and left.

His longtime love for Angela choked his throat. Offering to help Wil was the least he could do in her memory.

Agnes thought her life would be easier with only herself to worry about. She could go back to being a midwife. But a new doctor arrived in town and his wife was a midwife also and women wanted to go to this couple for complete care. The domestic chores she offered were expanded to cleaning homes as well as the washing and ironing. Her days were long and terribly tiring, but she resolutely kept trying to find any kind of work. When her malnourished body began to fail her, she wanted to give up, but didn't know how.

Agnes went to the General Store to ask Mr. Emerson if anyone had left a request for her services. She waited in the doorway while a thin boy talked to the shopkeeper about work. "I'll run errands – I'll sweep up - I'll put things away on your shelves. Please Mr. Emerson. I'm a good worker."

The owner shook his head. "Sorry, Jesse."

The boy's look of resignation shook Agnes to her soul. She had heard "Sorry" so many, many times when she asked for work. How could anyone say "No" to such a helpless boy? "Young man," she called as he passed her on his way out.

He turned. "You mean me?"

"Yes, you. What's your name?"

"Jesse Keller, Ma'am."

"Where do you live?"

The boy was hesitant. "Nowhere, Ma'am. I have no home."

Agnes thought she couldn't bear his polite and honest answers. No sass, no anger. "Jesse, why don't you walk with me and maybe we can discuss a plan that would do us both good."

And so it was that Jesse Keller came to live with Agnes Johnson in the attic space that had been Wil's. They shared simple meals. He helped her with heavy work and ran errands. She welcomed another person in the house even though they talked little. Keeping body and soul together didn't seem quite so unbearable with this boy who never complained nor got in trouble.

Agnes became quite fond of Jesse.

But he would never know it.

CHAPTER 32

S KY FIRE LAY prone on the butte and gazed on the circle of tepees in the valley below. He mumbled to himself as he took long swallows from a jug of whiskey, a habit he had acquired in earnest. "I hate the one who has taken my wife into his tepee, but now I shall use his ability as a scout to end my search for Kangee Kohana." Another swig as he scanned the scene below trying to identify Standing Warrior. "Why did I ever try to rely on scouts with no skill when the greatest of them all can lead me?" He swished the burning liquid around in the jug and again lifted it to his lips. "Surely he has kept a watchful eye on Kangee Kohana. Kimimela Weeko and Ehawee would want reports that their father is still alive."

He squinted his eyes to look again through the haze of liquor. Nowhere could he see Standing Warrior. But there! He recognized the two sisters among the many women going about their work. "Ah, now it begins," he said, relishing his plans. "I will easily capture my divorced wife. When I threaten to torture her, Ozuye Najin will lead me to the old man in order to save her. Then I will return to being a leader in a tribe like the one in the valley below." He scooted back and staggered to his horse. "Kimimela Weeko and Ehawee never change their morning routine. I shall be waiting."

Ever since the two sisters had lived in adjacent tepees, it had been their habit to go together to bathe in the early morning hours. Laughing Maiden would bring her little children. When Pretty Butterfly was Sky Fire's wife she had no children to bathe, but now, as second wife to Standing Warrior, she had two sons to carry with her.

On this morning Laughing Maiden had her second and third children, but her eldest son went to the boys' pool to join his friends. The women chose a shallow pool so they could let the little ones play in the water without fear. Pretty Butterfly's baby was taken from the cradle board and laid on a soft deer skin. He kicked his feet and chortled with glee as his mother splashed and rubbed him with the fresh water.

The women trusted one another to watch over the four infants while they took turns going to the women's bathing pool to freshen themselves and visit with their neighbors. Pretty Butterfly was trying to teach her older son to walk in the shallow water when a large shadow passed over her shoulder. Could Laughing Maiden be returning so soon? She looked up, into the enraged eyes of her former husband.

"Mahpee Paytah!" was all she could say before a leather gag was thrust into her mouth. She struggled as her hands and feet were quickly tied. Sky Fire threw her across his shoulder and ran into the woods where he tossed her across the back of his waiting black stallion. He secured her twisting body like the carcass of a slain deer. Springing up behind her, they rode away like the wind. The four babies continued to splash the water without noticing they were alone.

Once Sky Fire reached a safe distance, he dismounted, dragging Pretty Butterfly to the ground. He lashed her to a tree, left the gag in her mouth, and blindfolded her eyes. Then Sky Fire galloped back to the pool.

Laughing Maiden returned to give Pretty Butterfly her time at the women's bathing pool, but her sister was nowhere to be seen. She called but there was no answer. Something had happened. Pretty Butterfly would never have left the little ones alone. She looked at the ground and saw signs of a struggle and her heart beat faster. "Oh no!"

With the stealth that he had used to capture Pretty Butterfly, Sky Fire crept up to the second mother from behind. As fast as a lightning strike, she felt a sharp blade at her throat. A deep, guttural voice whispered, "Ehawee, I should use this to pay you back for allowing your sister to leave my tepee and share yours."

She knew that voice! "Mahpee Paytah! What do you want of me?"

"Take a message to your husband. I have Kimimela Weeko. She is hidden in a remote place. I shall not be merciful when I finally kill her. Unless...." And he swung the frightened woman around to face him. "Unless Ozuye Najin meets me on the bluff at sunrise tomorrow and leads me to Kangee Kohana. Do you understand?"

She trembled. "Yes, you will kill my sister unless my husband helps you find my father. But he is not here. He has gone and I don't know when he will return!"

"Then I shall meet him when the sun rises twice. If he is not there, I shall find pleasure in torturing your sister who disgraced me."

He put the knife back in the sheath and snatched up her smallest baby. "If I hear you scream for help when I leave, the child dies. If you are silent you will find your daughter along my trail." Sky Fire disappeared into the trees and returned to his black stallion which he had tied nearby. He easily sprang to its back, holding the baby upside down by one foot. The child was screaming loudly when he tossed it to the ground a short distance away.

Sky Fire galloped back to Pretty Butterfly. She knew it was hopeless to struggle as he released her from the tree without removing the gag, or blindfold, or ropes which bound her hands and feet. He threw her onto the horse and swung up in back of her. The village was soon left far behind.

Laughing Maiden could not utter a sound for fear of Sky Fire's threat. The terror of what had just happened to her and the child choked her throat. The thought of what lay in store for her sister made tears run down her cheek. The stories told about this renegade were so horrific as to strike her dumb. Her oldest son came from the boy's bathing pool and saw his mother's frightened face. "What is it?" he asked.

Now that she was sure Sky Fire couldn't hear her, she shouted to him, "Look after the babies!" Then she rushed in the direction Sky Fire had taken. In less than a half mile she found her third child lying in the grass screaming, but unhurt. She clutched the little girl to her breast and wept.

*   *   *   *   *   *

After several hours of riding, Sky Fire came to an abandoned soddy that he had used as a hideout on many occasions. Here he kept a cache of food and whiskey. He grinned as he remembered his gang of renegades raiding this homestead. They had captured a pretty young girl and kept her for their pleasure for several months. She might have lived longer as their whore if she had not been killed by his own arrow when she tried to escape. He would make sure this woman, who now called herself second wife of Standing Warrior, would not try anything so foolish.

Sky Fire pulled Pretty Butterfly off the horse and dropped her to the ground like a dead prairie chicken. He dragged her by her long, thick braids through the door hanging on its hinges and propped her against a wall. He took off the blindfold and she looked around with terror in her eyes.

"You wonder what is happening?" he said to Pretty Butterfly as he pulled the cork from the whiskey jug. "You are ransom for a very valuable prize which the man you now call your husband will deliver to me." He took a long swig of the brew and heaved a sigh of satisfaction. He then pulled a large knife from his leg sheath.

"Since you divorced me in such a shameful manner, I will now shame you." Pretty Butterfly whimpered as she imagined his revenge. Her eyes were beseeching which gave Sky Fire sadistic pleasure. "If ever you return to the village it will be without that lovely hair which you brush and wash so carefully." With giant slashes he cut the tresses from her head until her scalp bled. Her gagged voice was a cry of pain.

"This is only the beginning." He grabbed her braids and whacked her with them like whips. Tears flowed down her bruised cheeks.

"Now that I have robbed you of your beauty I will tell you why. The scout who shares your sleep robe will lead me to your father."

Pretty Butterfly's eyes went wide. She vigorously shook her head, No!

"Oh yes, he will do this gladly when he learns that you will be tortured if he refuses." Sky Fire laughed with a deep, guttural outburst.

"But while I wait two sunrises for this message to be given him by your sister, I shall exercise a husband's right to enjoy his wife's body – for you are still my squaw, Kimimela Weeko, no matter what you have done to divorce me. What a pleasure it will be to know you once again." He ripped off her dress.

As he untied her legs she twisted her body to and fro trying to avoid him and he laughed. "My little wild cat!" She thrashed her tied arms trying to hit him. "I shall not release your hands for they might claw me. I will not remove the gag from your mouth for your teeth could bite me. If you try to kick me…" The look of a killer came over his face. Pretty Butterfly immediately stopped her struggling. She did not want to die.

Night fell. Sky Fire had exhausted his prowess. He downed the last of the whiskey.

"I shall exercise a husband's privilege with you again – very soon," he slurred as he pushed Pretty Butterfly to the wall. She lay still, not even looking at him. The horror of what was happening must be held tight within herself. He tipped the jug to be sure it was empty, rolled over and collapsed on his back. The woman would still be there tomorrow. He needed to get some sleep and regain his vigor.

*   *   *   *   *   *

Standing Warrior felt renewed following his visit with his father-in-law and the boy. They were surviving very well alone in the wilderness. Their strength became his. As he returned to his village, Standing Warrior would need every bit of that strength.

He emerged from the hills leading Laughing Maiden's brown pack horse which he had exchanged for the handsome appaloosa. To his astonishment his first wife was outside the circle of tepees, frantically searching the skyline as if looking for him. When he was recognized she ran as fast as her legs could carry her. "Come quickly," she shouted from a distance.

Standing Warrior galloped his horse to met her. "Tell me why you run to greet me."

"Something terrible has happened at the bathing pool," she gasped. "I came and found the four little ones alone. Kimimela Weeko has been abducted by Mahpee Paytah! He threatens to kill her if you do not lead him to my father."

Standing Warrior reeled. Not since he had witnessed the slaughter of Brave Eagle's three children at the hands of the soldier had he felt such anger boil within him. Quickly, he handed her the jaw-thong of the pack animal. "Take care of your horse. I must go quickly before any trail fades that I might follow." He sped off to the bathing pool at a full gallop.

As Standing Warrior studied the area around the pool it was not difficult for him to surmise what had happened. The scout's sharp eyes saw traces of a person being dragged. His sensitive nose could detect the fragrance of his second wife.

He closed his eyes, reached deep into himself and drew upon every lesson, every skill he had ever learned over his lifetime. He would follow this trail, rescue Pretty Butterfly… he would find Sky Fire and…

Dusk brought dark shadows that equaled Standing Warrior's fury. There in the dim light, the scout saw an old soddy. A big, black stallion, which he recognized immediately, was cropping grass. Standing Warrior dismounted and looped the jaw-thong over a bush. With the stealth of a mountain lion he crept closer. His perfect hearing recognized whimpers, muttered words, but no cries of torture.

The door to the soddy hung open. The light inside was dim, but his eyes were trained to see even in the dark. The woman pinned to the floor was definitely Pretty Butterfly. The naked man crushing her was unquestionably Sky Fire.

With a war cry that made the dirt walls tremble, Standing Warrior leapt into the room, slammed into the prone body of Sky Fire, flipping him over and onto his back. His hand shot forward, the blade of his tomahawk pressed against Sky Fire's throat while he wrapped his legs around his torso, pinning both arms to his sides. Sky Fire knew that any struggling would only cause the blade to slice off his head.

With clenched teeth and wild eyes, Standing Warrior lowered his face to within a breath of Sky Fire. "I could end your miserable life this moment. But that would not be sufficient. Your punishment must equal the atrocities that you have done." Standing Warrior used the rope that had bound Pretty Butterfly's legs to truss Sky Fire.

He held both hands out to his wife and gently raised her to sit beside him. He carefully removed the gag and cut her bonds. She pointed to her torn dress and he slipped it over her head. He looked into her eyes. Without speaking, Standing Warrior assured her that no further harm would come to her. Ever.

Sky Fire looked at Standing Warrior with contemptuous resignation. "Untie me and let me die as a warrior with your spear in my heart."

"Never" said Standing Warrior. "You have disgraced the honor of every brave warrior who kills only for his tribe or his family."

He raised the tomahawk. "You will never again lift a tomahawk, or draw a bow, or let another spear fly." He swung the blunt side of the weapon and instantly broke every bone in both Sky Fire's arms. The renegade screamed.

"Never again will you go looking for an honorable old man who has the courage of the wolf to love and protect a boy whom you rejected." The tomahawk head crashed against the kneecaps, then calves and thighs. Sky Fire wailed in pain.

Standing Warrior looked at Pretty Butterfly, feeling a love deeper than any he thought possible. "My wife has strength you cannot begin to imagine. She will gradually forget you and what you have done, for I will give her a beautiful life, day after day, and she will live in the present of each day, not the past. But you will never forget this day – from this day on you will no longer be able to torture any woman as you have my wife."

Standing Warrior's tomahawk slashed the body of Sky Fire one more time blade side down, not to crush or shatter, but to slice and sever. "This is the day you lost your masculinity." Sky Fire didn't hear Standing Warrior for he had lost consciousness.

Standing Warrior held Pretty Butterfly to his chest. "Are you all right?" he asked, stroking her cropped head. She nodded, but could not yet utter a word. "Come, we shall go back. If he dies, so be it. If he lives, he will wish he were dead. Either way, he is nothing to us."

After lifting Pretty Butterfly onto his own horse, Standing Warrior mounted Sky Fire's fiery black stallion which he could control with his quirt. She slumped forward but forced herself to raise her head to ask, "Are your sons all right?"

"Yes. Ehawee cares for them." They rode silently back to their precious children.

Upon their return to their village, the scout dismounted the stallion. The horse broke free from his grip and with a mighty whinney it reared up on its hind legs and galloped back into the forest from whence they had come.

CHAPTER 33

FOR THE NEXT two years Kincade was so busy growing up that he hardly realized that Swift Raven was growing old. They moved slowly when they traveled. They stayed longer in the camps. Even the mysterious messages from the raven to move on were not followed immediately, but perhaps several days later. Although Swift Raven knew he was no longer the spry octogenarian who chased after buffalo, his determination to train the boy in the Indian Way never lessened.

The horse Lightning had been well cared for, but Swift Raven knew that every horse needed to bond with its owner. Swift Raven taught Kincade to curry its coat, mane and tail using only the boy's fingers rather than the harshness of tools. "If the horse feels your hands, it will know your heart," said Swift Raven. Daily he was to check the hooves, mouth and nostrils. It was totally Kincade's responsibility to take Lightning to the best grass and pure water.

Swift Raven also taught Kincade to leap on Lightning's back. "Become one with the horse," he said. Swift Raven rode stride for stride alongside the boy, instructing with both actions and words. Kincade loved to ride bareback as the quivering horse flesh rippled beneath him like fast water running over smooth rock. In the days to follow, Kincade learned to guide his horse using only the pressure of his knees. Swift Raven knew that when the time came for

Kincade to shoot from horseback, he would no longer need to hold the jaw-thong. His arms would be free for letting arrows fly from his bow. "Killing deer and antelope will be more fun when I am galloping," Kincade shouted to his partner.

As the boy became more proficient with twisting and turning, Swift Raven found himself getting dizzy when he rode alongside. Kincade's skills as a horseman had begun to exceed his own. "I shall watch from here," he said as he slid to the ground, feeling proud of the boy's accomplishments.

Kincade wheeled to halt in front of him. "I think I am ready to kill a buffalo!"

"You think the wolves are hungry again?" Swift Raven laughed, wondering if Kincade actually could down such a large beast. But it was not yet time, so he shook his head. "No, our prey should be something we can completely consume ourselves. To waste is not the Indian Way."

"Then I shall kill a rabbit – you eat so little now it should satisfy your hunger."

That evening Swift Raven sat cross legged looking beyond the fire's low flames at Kincade. What a change ten years had made. He was no longer a boy, yet not quite a man. Kincade stood head and shoulders above the little man who had known more than ninety winters. Swift Raven was not sure if the boy was growing faster than spring's prairie grass, or if his aging body had shrunk considerably from his days of being a mighty scout.

The most remarkable change was in Kincade's face. The fire-light showed the boy's soft fuzz of mustache and beard. But that was not what struck Swift Raven. It was Kincade's look of self-confidence and his excitement for living that glowed from within his deep blue eyes. Although Kincade's tanned muscles were not yet manly, they were strong and handsome to behold when the boy went bare-chested.

Swift Raven was proud, but not of himself for having fashioned and directed the person squatting before the fire. He was proud of Kincade for evolving into the unusual person he had become. Whether the Great Spirit or Kincade himself had molded the young man seated at the edge of the fire, Swift Raven's eyes saw nothing but perfection. But the feeling soon disappeared as if swept up by the fire's smoke. Suddenly, Swift Raven saw a reflection of himself, and with it, his own limitations.

This was not enough. It would not do. Not for this boy for whom he cared so deeply.

"This is not right," Swift Raven said out loud.

"What is not right, Old Indian?"

How could he explain it? He looked at this young man who meant everything to him. "You are walking in my shadow."

"And I am honored to do so," answered Kincade.

"No," said Swift Raven. "You are not me. The shadow you follow must be your own." Swift Raven stood, looking directly into Kincade's blue eyes. "Are you ready to make your own shadow without anyone to guide or protect you?"

Kincade looked at his companion with pride. "I have had the best teacher. Why should I not have the necessary skills to face any adventure with only my own mind and body?" Kincade rose to face Swift Raven. "If you wish to test me, Old Indian, I am ready."

Swift Raven smiled for this was the answer he wanted. But was Kincade's bravado only that – bravado - or could the boy actually walk in his own footsteps?

"Tomorrow, Kincade. We shall see tomorrow." And with that Swift Raven went to his sleeping robe.

The sun had barely left its nightly hiding place when Kincade and Swift Raven stirred from their robes, walking side by side to the stream, splashing water over their bodies. Kincade wondered if Old Indian remembered their conversation of the previous evening. Then the boy laughed, thinking to himself, "Old Indian never forgets anything!"

The two returned to their camp, fanned the nearly exhausted coals into flame, and then ate a meal of meat and vegetable roots in silence. The two finished. Kincade practiced The Wait, knowing that Old Indian would speak only when he was ready. Eventually, Swift Raven nodded, and spoke to the boy.

"You may take three things with you. Think carefully before you choose."

Without hesitating Kincade said, "First I want you. Second I want Lightning. Third I want the raven who guides us."

The old man shook his head, chuckling. The boy had a quick sense of humor. "You must do without companionship – human, animal, or feathered friend."

Kincade smiled at Old Indian, feeling good at seeing his mentor's happiness. The boy knew this test was important, so he thought carefully before replying in earnest. "I choose to take a knife, a water-sac..."

"Empty water-sac," Swift Raven interrupted.

"Yes, empty," wishing to himself that Old Indian had missed the distinction. "And a light summer robe."

"Why do you decide on these three?"

"For food, for water, for shelter. All else will be provided by the land around me."

Swift Raven nodded. "Wise," was all he said. Then he glanced at the sky. "We leave before the sun touches those tree tops. Get ready."

Kincade put his knife into a leg sheath, fastened a water-sac to his loincloth strap, and tied a light robe around his waist. Then he stood in the center of their campsite and looked in the four directions, memorizing all the features which could lead him back.

The butte to the north was not far away. It was distinguished by several deep ravines which must have carried spring run-offs in three giant waterfalls. Extending to the east was the vast aspen grove in which they had set up camp. On the south was the stream whose current flowed from west to east. At the edge of the aspen on the west was a dense forest of conifers.

Having memorized his bearings, Kincade led Lightning to where Swift Raven waited outside the tepee.

"Do you make me walk or ride?"

"Your feet would teach you too much if you walked. You will ride until the spot where I leave you."

"Won't I see where you are leading me if I ride?"

"No." Swift Raven held up a piece of soft leather. "I will bind this over your eyes."

"And what if I can peek under it just a little?"

Swift Raven smiled. "You will not cheat, for this adventure is to prove you are a man, not a little boy playing a game."

Now it was Kincade's turn to smile. Old Indian had answers to everything. Kincade wondered if he would return to Swift Raven with new answers of his own. "I am ready."

"Take with you one more thing." He handed Kincade a large, green stick with the bark peeled off. The Old Indian held a similar one in his other hand.

"At each sunrise we both will cut a notch in the stick. I will expect to see you again after five notches." Kincade accepted the stick. "Now, lean down so I can cover your eyes."

Kincade did not need to see to nimbly jump onto Lightning's back. When he reached for the jaw-thong, he realized Old Indian held it, leading Lightning behind his own mount.

The adventure had begun. Kincade felt confident. If he could not use his eyes he would start immediately to use his other senses. Perhaps they would serve him even better. The boy turned inward, knowing that smell, sound, touch and even taste were not easily disguised, whereas sometimes the eyes deceived.

Another smile crossed Kincade's young face. This was going to be fun.

As the two rode, Kincade listened to the rustling of aspen leaves. Their quake grew softer and more distant as the horses moved forward, soon giving way to the sticky smell of pine resin carried on a slight breeze. He knew the direction Old Indian was taking: West.

They progressed slowly. Kincade counted the number of times they went up a steep slope and down a deep gully. "Once up, once down, up again." They must now be on a plateau. He heard the gurgle of running water. This was not the same gentle steam that flowed near their campsite for when the horses were lead across Kincade felt the splash of deeper water upon his legs.

The hoof falls of the horses usually indicated forest undergrowth, but there was one stretch which puzzled Kincade. Old Indian must be following some sort of trail. The boy would hear the swish of tall grasses, and then the grating of sand and packed dirt paired with the kicking up of small stones, the swish of much shorter grass, a second grating of sand, packed dirt and small stone that matched the first, and the second swish of taller grasses. All the sounds occurred within a very short distance. Drawing upon everything he had ever heard over his years with Old Indian, Kincade could not picture what they had just crossed. These sounds were unlike any he had heard, so he memorized them. On his return to their camp, Kincade's ears would recognize these strange sounds again. Only then would his eyes identify the source of whatever it was that he and Old Indian were crossing.

Kincade's nose twitched. The boy could smell a herd of buffalo. He knew that the smell did not reveal how close the beasts were, as the animals' noxious excrement could carry for miles on a slight breeze.

Old Indian and Kincade rode on in silence, the boy using every bit of training given him over the years, gaining a new appreciation for the lessons he had received from the wisdom of Old Indian.

The sun had ceased to warm Kincade's back. It now beat down on his chest and face. They had come a great distance following the sun as it arched over their heads and descended towards the western horizon.

Swift Raven came to a halt. "I leave you here," he said. "Slide off your horse."

"May I remove the mask now?"

"Not until you hear the call of the wolf," said Swift Raven. "This will be my own voice signaling you." Kincade slid from his horse, feeling a mat of moss and fallen pine needles beneath his moccasins.

"I will see you after five sunrises," said Swift Raven. "Remember to marvel at the wonders all around you. Accept those that will be useful to you. Imitate nature as best a man can." Then he was gone.

Kincade remained perfectly still, immersed in the patience of The Wait. Finally he heard a distant howl.

The boy tore off the soft blindfold and looked around. He was not surprised at a forest of stubby pinion and juniper trees around him. What did surprise him was not seeing the prints of hooves to indicate which way Old Indian had left. And even though he walked for some distance in every direction there were no horse droppings anywhere within sight. He laughed. Old Indian would not make this adventure easy.

Kincade decided he would not go further this first night. He scratched an arrow in the direction of the sun closing its arc into the western sky. In the morning he would watch for the sun's rise so he would know the direction of east. Already Kincade felt secure with the familiar things Old Indian had taught him.

His excitement staved off hunger. Knowing he must remain strong and alert, Kincade decided to quench his thirst by picking the ripe berries he had seen when looking for Old Indian's departure path. The bushes held many of the red berries, and he squashed them in his mouth savoring the juices running down his throat. Chewing them would only leave their million seeds stuck in his teeth.

There were also clusters of white berries. To the unlearned, those berries might deceive the eyes and tempt the palate. But Old Indian had warned Kincade long ago that these could be poisonous. "You must use your eyes to find the truth, Kincade" he would teach. "Do not allow anything to deceive you. All the answers to all the questions may be found through the eyes."

Having his fill of red berries, Kincade gathered pinion nuts, collecting a small pile for his morning meal. It was a warm evening. No fire was necessary. Kincade found a patch of wild grass. Kneeling, the boy gathered up a fist full of small stones. He threw them in a wide arc across the grasses. Their fall would stir any rattlesnake resting there. Hearing nothing, smelling no scent of the creature, Kincade shook out his robe, spreading it over the soft grass.

He stretched out, placed his hands behind his head and sighed deeply as the sky turned black. The boy felt at home in the wild. He had never known anything else. The sky had always been his roof, the land beneath Kincade's body a pallet and a comfort.

The boy searched the twinkling canopy overhead for the star Old Indian taught was a constant companion and guide. This star was always fixed. Kincade smiled, finding it easily, a bright bold finger pointing north. The opposite direction would be south.

Kincade rolled to his side and fumbled for the stick Old Indian had given him. He tucked one end under his robe. The opposite end Kincade pointed towards the star. Then he sighed again with total contentment. Kincade was alone, but he was not lonely. This trait was inside Kincade's heart.

He closed his eyes and slept soundly.

CHAPTER 34

KINCADE AWAKENED AT dawn and shook out the soft robe, once again tying it around his waist. Then he began searching in the half-light for any plants with leaves which might have caught the night's dew. One by one he licked up any moisture, being careful not to cut his tongue on sharp edges. It was hardly a thirst quenching drink but at least his mouth was no longer dry. He sat cross-legged to eat the pinion nuts he had gathered and to plan his day. That reminded him to put the first notch on the stick Old Indian had given him to mark the passage of time.

First he would find a stream and fill his water-sac. He tried to orient his present location to the stream they had crossed the day before. All he could remember was that it lay to the east, probably beyond a valley and up a steep ridge. He looked around as if expecting Old Indian or the raven to point the way. No, he reminded himself, and he set out running toward the beautiful red sunrise.

Kincade counted his running steps. Then he jogged the same number. Finally he walked and counted twice as many, breathing deeply. He continued this routine as the eastern sky left its night colors behind to become a bright blue. He felt good for the air was scented with woody fragrances. The sky held fluffy, white clouds, and the loam beneath his feet was soft and didn't push through his moccasins. Perhaps his third choice should have been to bring extra moccasins. These soles would become thin in five days. But he had chosen the soft robe instead and it was better than sleeping on bare ground last night. Pausing to swallow, he wished that his second choice had been a full water-sac, not an empty one. It bounced against his leg, taunting his growing thirst.

He kept telling himself that there was no point dwelling on things he would have to go without. Yet every time Kincade slowed to walk he looked in all directions, hoping to see a place for getting water. Was there any cactus he could pierce with his knife? No. Was there sand which he could dig into until water seeped to the surface? No. Would there be rain before the day was over? He looked at the benevolent sky and knew that was not going to happen. He felt his tongue sticking to the top of his mouth, so he sucked on a round rock to create saliva. That didn't help very much.

With every disappointment, Kincade felt more thirst, but he refused to panic. What had Old Indian taught him that could serve him now? He would practice The Wait and find understanding.

He stopped his running, jogging and walking and sat down to direct his full attention to the problem. Of course! Animals needed water. Where had he seen or heard animals? Then he remembered yesterday. Buffalo! He had smelled buffalo! The beasts always roamed where they could get water. All he had to do was locate the herd he had smelled the day before.

How could he find them? The scent was gone. His nose was of no use. Neither did his eyes see buffalo. Then he remembered what Old Indian had done when he slew the buffalo years before – he had heard the beasts. Old Indian had put his ear to the ground and listened.

Kincade built a small pile of stones to mark the spot where he sat and the easterly direction he had been headed. Then he walked north about a half mile before stopping and putting his ear to the ground. He heard nothing. He continued west in the direction he had just traversed and stooped to listen again. Nothing. He circled south, stopped, and pressed his ear to the earth. He sighed and stood up quite discouraged. He was almost ready to continue back to his starting place when he noticed that long clouds had filled the sky and a sudden breeze swept across his face. The wind had shifted directions. There it was! The distinctive odor he had noticed when he was blindfolded. Now he knew that a herd of buffalo was not far to the south. He began to run in that direction.

Two hours of running, jogging, and walking and Kincade spotted several hundred of the shaggy animals peacefully grazing. His eyes frantically searched for their water hole. The herd spread out evenly across the plains with the exception of one place where a greater concentration gathered. That must be it. Kincade felt lucky that the water hole wasn't near the center of the herd. Kincade would need to approach the hole from downwind so the buffalo would not sense his presence and panic.

He threw the light robe over his head and shoulders and slumped to appear as buffalo-like as possible. Old Indian had told him, "They have poor eyes but excellent noses." Perhaps he could fool the buffalo if they just didn't smell him. Most of the herd was feeding in the grasses. Kincade cautiously crept toward what he hoped would be a large pool of water surrounded by sand and pebbles. His thirst leapt out ahead of him and he envisioned scooping up water and gulping handfull after handfull.

When he came close his hopes were dashed. He stared at very brown water, stirred up by the buffalo from a muddy bottom. If he drank this he would never return to Old Indian in five days – maybe never. Why hadn't he insisted on carrying a full water-sac!

Like a daydream, Kincade imagined water coursing over his body, cooling the heat, soothing his thirst. Tears formed behind his eyes. Then Kincade shook free of the tormenting image. Old

Indian said, "A real man only cries when an enemy kills his relative – that is the Indian Way." Kincade was on this adventure to prove himself a real man - a man who knows the Indian Way. He would need to accept this challenge – not in an easy way – but in a different way.

The buffalo grazing nearby still had not noticed the intruder, or if they had they weren't paying him much attention. So he slipped the robe off his shoulders and looked around. How could he purify the water? He thought of all the streams where he and Old Indian had raised their tepee. The best tasting water had rushed over rocks and stones, sand bars, and even marshy, willow-filled eddies. Nature had scrubbed the water and made it sweet to drink. That was what he must do – wash the water - but how?

Closing his eyes, Kincade thought of the lessons he had learned over the years. Then, an idea appeared. Just before he found the herd he had passed through a small grove of white trees which had strips of bark peeling off their trunks. The more he thought about it, the more he believed he could carefully wrap this bark into a large cone with a small hole left in the bottom. He visualized securing it with the strap of the water-sac, then filling the cone with layers of sand, small pebbles, and sweet grass - if he could find any that hadn't been trampled.

Yes, this might work. He would pass the brown water through this filter into the water-sac and hope it would come out clear enough to drink. It would take time for he only had his hand to scoop up the water, but if this worked Old Indian would be so proud of him. He could hardly wait to crawl back to the birch grove and cut off the right piece of bark with his knife.

Painstakingly, Kincade filled his water-sac using the filtered cone. Once the sac was full and Kincade knew he could drink, his thirst left him, but he was curious. He tipped the sac to his lips. The water may have looked clear but it had a strange taste. The boy spit out the liquid without swallowing. He feared the foul water would make him sick. Fine for buffalo, but not for him.

Securing the full water-sac to his side, Kincade walked back to the starting place where he had made the small pile of stones. He picked the red berries and squashed the juice slowly in his mouth. It wasn't the long drink he had hoped for, but it was enough. Tonight he would sleep where leaves with morning dew would be plentiful. Hopefully tomorrow he would find the stream and get enough fresh, pure water to last the next four days.

Kincade patted his full water-sac with pride. He wouldn't swallow the liquid but he could probably rinse his mouth and spit it out without getting sick. "But only if I'm really desperate," he told himself, and then he added, "I wonder if buffalos can spit?" This thought sent him laughing. Life was good. He had met his first problem in the Indian Way.

CHAPTER 35

THE DAY OF the second sunrise dawned gray and Kincade was glad he had marked the easterly direction with stones for the sun was not visible through the thick clouds. He notched Old Indian's calendar stick and prepared to run and jog and walk on. He had not gone far when soft rain began to fall. A wind made it rapidly gain momentum and before he realized it hail was pounding his head and shoulders. It felt marvelous! Like strong fingers massaging his weary body. Kincade stood in the midst of the battering and threw a challenge to the icy pellets. With his arms outstretched he yelled, "You may pound me but you won't drive me down. I shall…I shall…" and suddenly he knew what he would do. He whipped the soft robe from around his waist and spread it over the ground. "I shall catch your little icy balls and turn them into water!"

The robe was quickly covered with hail and without waiting for the storm to cease, Kincade dumped out the buffalo water and dropped icy stones one by one into the water-sac until he could fill it no more. He put several in his mouth and gratefully sucked the cold moisture. "Thank you, Spirit of the Sky! Thank you, thank you!" he chanted as he danced around and around. Then before the pellets melted and soaked the robe, he shook off the remainder and draped the skin over his head and shoulders. It would give him some protection until the storm passed. He huddled under the low branches of a juniper tree and practiced The Wait.

Hour after hour the wind howled and the rain dripped through the branches. Kincade shivered. He was miserably cold and uncomfortable. Darkness descended and fear crept over him. What if he couldn't find his way back to the snug tepee and the warmth of a buffalo robe? Worst of all, what if Old Indian didn't look for him should he not find his way back in three more days? Finally he fell into a troubled sleep.

When Kincade awakened he could see sunlight pushing through the eastern clouds. The air was heavy with moisture. He crawled out from under the juniper and shook the robe hoping the rain hadn't soaked through. It had. But the leather was soft enough that he could ring out the wetness, again and again, and finally he tied it around his waist. He marked the third notch in the calendar stick and started towards the sunrise.

Kincade's energy was draining for he and Old Indian ate meat every day. It could be fresh killed, then roasted on a spit, baked in a pit, or boiled in a bag. In the winter there was pemmican and jerky. He was growing very tired of eating only wild fruits and nuts. He grumbled as he trudged along through wet foliage and muddy footing. He wished he had chosen his bow and arrow to bring along. If he saw a deer, or even a rabbit, he couldn't kill it. The adventure was ceasing to be fun, in fact it was even becoming alarming. His stomach growled, being deprived of rib-sticking sustenance.

Suddenly a wild Tom turkey scurried from the undergrowth, frightened by his footsteps. Kincade's spirits rose from the depths to the heights. Here was meat, if only he could catch it.

Kincade reached and lunged. The turkey frantically flapped its wings to escape, but the feathers had become soaked in the hail storm and useless for flying. This didn't stop the bird from running on long legs, gobbling in a terrified fit. Its bright red wattle was flapping as it dodged this way and that with Kincade right behind it. Several times the boy almost grabbed it, but the Tom knew his life was in peril and he dashed over and under rocks and bushes, his red head turning white and then bright blue as his panic increased. Kincade was out of breath before he finally grabbed the tail feathers and pinned the Tom between his legs. He panted his blessing: "Thank you for giving your life so that my hunger pangs can cease." He drew his knife from the scabbard and lopped off its head. He let the body go and it raced around with wings flapping and blood spurting from the neck. Finally the Tom went limp in a soggy heap.

Kincade had no intention of eating raw turkey, but as he looked around, he realized the ground was far too wet to build a cooking fire. "I shall carry the bird and perhaps soon I'll come to a place that the storm did not drench."

He tried to lift the wet carcass but it proved to be incredibly heavy. Kincade rubbed his chin and considered his options. "I shall pluck the turkey here and now and cut out the edible meat. That should make it easy to carry." He had watched Old Indian do this before. He would have to remember if he wanted meat for dinner. He turned the carcass onto its back and went to work pulling, jerking, tugging, yanking out the soft breast feathers. Those that weren't too wet he stuck into the soles of his moccasins which were beginning to wear thin. Old Indian had cleaned the whole turkey, for both of them could eat it all. Kincade would only take what he alone could eat. Perhaps he would try to call the wolves to finish it off.

The naked breast was soon exposed and carefully Kincade peeled back the skin with his knife. The fat white meat lay on each side of the breast bone, easy to cut away. Kincade looked at the mutilated body of the bird. Many of the long feathers were beautiful – iridescent green and russet and copper. "Too bad I won't be keeping some of these," he said to himself. He stroked his fingers along the most colorful. "Old Indian would tell me to make a war bonnet with them." He laughed. "A remembrance of my running battle with this turkey." Everything he did reminded him of the fun he shared with the companion he had left behind.

Kincade wrapped the breast filets in leaves and put them in the center of the sleeping robe. He tied up the corners and fastened it to a long stick, resting the knapsack on his shoulder. The day was half gone. He ran, jogged, and walked.… ran, jogged, and walked while the turkey meat seemed to get heavier and heavier. Hours passed. Finally the dampness on the ground diminished, the bushes and trees looked totally dry as if not a drop of moisture had fallen for weeks. He breathed a sigh of relief as he entered a small clearing. It was time to start a fire and cook a good meal.

He put the burden down. Old Indian made building a fire look easy. So he set out to find all the things he would need. He looked around for a slab of dry wood on which to build his fire and a nice round sagebrush stick for the twirler. He would need tiny wood shavings for tinder and he used his knife to cut and sliver dead bark from a fallen tree. He gathered small, dry twigs to gradually add once smoke began rising. Then he made a pile of larger pieces to add to small flames until they grew into big ones.

An hour later he was still twirling a makeshift stick and blowing onto dry bark chips. So many things he had taken for granted when living with Old Indian now seemed impossible to do. But he would not give up. His technique was lacking but he would not let depression take hold of him again. Finally smoke curled and with a whoop of joy he added the kindling and larger pieces one at a time. He had a fire! He had meat! Now he could eat a good meal!

Dozens – maybe hundreds – of times he and Old Indian had roasted meat on a spit. While the flames of the fire burned down, Kincade set about fashioning a rack. He cut two sturdy, forked sticks and planted them deep on each side of the fire. He stripped a third stick clean of bark and sharpened the end with his knife. The meat would be skewered on it and suspended between the other two. He was so engrossed in the project that time passed quickly and it was almost dark before he pierced both halves of the turkey breast and hung them over the glowing embers to cook.

Kincade's mouth watered as the meat sizzled and browned. He never remembered roasted meat smelling so good. He kept the fire going but never allowed flames to singe the bird. Every once in awhile he would break off a small piece that looked thoroughly cooked and almost burn his tongue tasting it. "No, just a little while longer," he had to tell himself, and he would turn the skewer to roast the opposite side. Finally the white meat tasted perfect and he carefully lifted the skewer off the rack and slid the meat onto the soft robe. He sat cross legged and sunk his teeth into the first meat he had eaten in days. He called into the wind, "Old Indian, I am such a good cook! Would you care to come here and share this meal with me?"

His mentor may have been unable to accept the boy's invitation, but another guest planned to attend the feast when she first smelled the aroma of roasting meat. She lumbered through the forest following her sensitive nose for several miles. Kincade jumped up as a female grizzly moved into the clearing where the boy ate, ready to fill her belly - invited or not.

Old Indian had once told Kincade a story about the bear. She was Guardian of The Place Of The Sunset - one of the seven directions. Although revered, the Indians called her Old Clumsy Foot. But Old Indian warned Kincade she was nothing of the sort. Deadly when provoked or confronted, she could outrun the fastest man, ripping him into shreds with claws longer than the boy's longest finger. She was not only to be respected, but given wide berth.

In the dim moonlight he could see the huge, silver-tipped animal rise up on hind legs and swing her head back and forth, locating the origin of the smell. Kincade tossed the piece he was eating towards her while slowly backing away from the light of the dying fire. The bear dropped to all fours to scavenge the piece of meat.

Kincade moved back as far as possible without alarming her. As Old Indian had instructed him in this situation, he lay prone on his stomach in a dark recess of the night, trying to look dead in spite of the trembling of every nerve in his body. He took one quick look at the advancing grizzly before covering his head with his arms. She appeared to be a young bear, but old enough to be smart in the ways of killing for food. He silently lifted his words to the Great Spirit. "Let me die bravely – in the Indian Way."

The grizzly quickly found the turkey meat and sat on her haunches to paw the pieces and slowly bite into them. She did not appear ravenous or in any particular hurry to leave once she'd eaten. Her grunts and growls were not menacing. She began prowling around, hunting for anything else to eat. Slowing his breathing to an absolute minimum, Kincade wondered how appetizing his unwashed body might smell. Would the dirt and sweat of the last few days be delicious or repugnant?

The bear came upon his still body. It was very hard for him to not move a muscle as she poked and pushed him with her nose, sniffing loudly. "Never appear to be a threat to a bear," Old Indian had told him. A threat! He was so weak with fear that he couldn't have swatted a mosquito, let alone a four hundred pound bear.

Her curiosity heightened. Perhaps she had never been this close to a human before. She brushed his body with her right claw, just a scratch, not deep enough to draw blood. Then she stepped on his back with her left foot and the mark of her five claws were left in his flesh. She growled through her bared teeth as if to bite. Kincade prepared to die.

The boy's Guardian Spirit must have spoken to the Guardian Of The Place Of The Sunset, for after a moment's consideration she shook her massive head and returned to circle the fire for any turkey she might have missed. Finding nothing more of interest, she ambled back into the forest and Kincade heard her grunting her way into the darkness.

The danger was over but he still lay motionless for a long time. He would not sleep tonight, even though the experiences of the day had left him exhausted. He did not wish to dream that he had been the grizzly's most satisfying meal.

CHAPTER 36

KINCADE MADE THE fourth notch on the calendar stick. If he were to prove himself a man, he had this day and the next to work his way back to Old Indian. He began running twice as far as he jogged and walked. Had his easterly direction been too far to the south or north? There was no way to know except to continue and look diligently for any signs that he might have identified when Old Indian led him away blindfolded. He went up slopes and down ravines, in and out of various evergreen stands. He sniffed the air and listened to the chatter of ground animals and songs of birds perched in the trees or flying overhead. Everything seemed monotonously the same, but he kept going.

Abruptly, he stopped. What was this? Not in all his years with Old Indian had Kincade seen anything like this. Then he realized that, although he hadn't seen it before, he had heard it before – once – four days ago when he was blindfolded - the swishing of grasses, grating of sand and dirt, kicking up of small rocks. He looked and looked. So this is what those sounds were.

It was a trail, in fact two trails, running parallel along a wide stretch of dirt. But what would be the point in that? Indians used trails through the wilderness, but they did not walk side by side on two trails but one behind the other on just one path. The dirt had been packed down, as if a hundred Indians had danced over it for weeks on end. Crushed stones were lying in the short grasses growing between the two trails. On each side, tall grasses stood untrammeled. Curiously these twin trails continued uninterrupted as far as Kincade could see – a never-ending line.

Kincade knelt down and tried to figure out what this could be. He had seen dried up streambeds this wide but here there were not any washed river rocks to indicate that water had flowed along this path. He remembered that he had once seen a wide, rocky path going down a hillside. Old Indian had explained that an avalanche of boulders had long ago cut a wide swath, tearing trees from roots as the rocks careened downward. But here, Kincade saw only flatness.

There were gouges on the two trails that looked like several snakes had slithered along on the ground without ever separating or getting closer together. Kincade ran his finger along the smooth ruts. They were wider and deeper than the lines the dragpoles made. Did a creature leave marks like this? He followed, hoping to see it.

Ahead he came to strange objects at the sides of this double trail. There was a wheel much larger than Kincade had ever imagined. The Indians made small wheels to hold scalps and to use as targets for throwing spears. The Dream Catcher given him by Old Indian was a still smaller wheel. Kincade went close to measure its size. This wheel was as large as his outstretched arms. What could such a big wheel be used for? Scalps? Games? It appeared to be broken. He walked on.

Further up the trail there was a large brown object which Kincade at first thought was a dead animal. As he got close he realized it was made of wood. He stopped to examine it closely. Similar but smaller shapes moved in an out of the larger one and things were inside. In a few were square, white leaves, only these leaves hadn't come from trees and they had a funny feel to them. Marks were all over them in straight lines. There were other strange objects like small sticks with black points.

What were they? He closed his eyes and tried to imagine their use. Sometimes Old Indian pulled a blackened stick out of the fire and drew an animal or symbol on a hide. But those were big sticks and these were so little. He rubbed the black point of one on a piece of the white leaf and it left a mark. He put them back in the little space and kept walking.

The next strange object had strips of wood all fastened together, two sides matching. Perhaps it was turned over, and if he straightened it…. Kincade put two curved pieces of wood on the bottom and a solid square in the middle and a ladder-like piece at the top.

He gasped. Somewhere in the back of his memory he remembered a woman holding him on such an object and rocking back and forth. She was humming. He almost caught the tune.

Kincade shook his head to clear the confusion he felt. The twin trails with these strange objects and distant memories were pulling him away from Old Indian. He must not let that happen – at least not until after all the notches had been cut on the calendar stick. He ran back in the direction from which he had come.

He didn't recognize the spot where he had come across the strange trail, so he just followed it toward the north, hoping that sooner or later he would get his orientation back to travel eastward. He hadn't gone far before he could hear a stream – gurgling water that he remembered his horse Lightning riding through. He must be on the right path at last!

He ran until he could see bright splashes over big river-rocks, cascades falling into pools, pussy-willows along the shoreline! He knew where he was! Hastily stripping off all his clothes, he jumped into the refreshing water. He laughed and tossed great sprays over his head and entire body. Had water ever felt so cool – so refreshing – so rejuvenating? He cupped his hands and drank greedy gulps, spitting it out between his lips and letting it drip down his chin.

For an hour he played and bathed himself. Then he crawled up the bank and lay on a patch of grass to dry himself in the sun. He soon fell asleep, relaxed, happy, and confident that this was the same stream where he and Old Indian had raised their tepee.

Kincade awakened in the blue of night. He had slept longer than the sun had traversed the sky. He sat up and groped for his clothes, his knife, his water-sac, his soft robe. All were there close by and he put them on. But it was too dark to travel more. He would wait for sunrise. Then he would mark the last notch on the calendar stick and before the next nightfall he would be back with Old Indian and hopefully a good supper with lots of meat.

He spread the soft robe by the stream whose gurgling lulled him back to sleep. Tomorrow would be a good day.

And a good day it was. Kincade followed the downward course of the water. There were a few times when large boulders made him leave the stream's bank but it was never difficult to come back to its rippling sound. He remembered clearly when Lightning had splashed through the streambed. How much had happened to him since then! He could hardly wait to tell Old Indian of his adventures and all he had learned.

He stopped, suddenly presented with another problem - another choice to be made. The stream divided, pouring into two smaller channels, one fork flowing to his right, the other to his left. Which should he follow? He sat on his haunches and practiced The Wait. But instead of getting understanding, he became confused as to the direction Old Indian had first taken. Had they left their campsite to go in a northerly or southerly direction? Or had they traveled directly west? His head started to spin with this dilemma. Then he stood and straightened his shoulders. He would follow the stream on his right. If this proved to be the wrong choice after a reasonable time walking he could backtrack and go to the left. That would be the Indian Way.

Kincade followed the right-hand stream bank and when it meandered through a large aspen grove he was sure he'd chosen correctly. Doggedly he went on, further and further until night overtook him and he could not see his way well enough to continue. Once again he lay down on the soft robe and counted the stars. He knew they were looking down on him as he looked up to them. He and the sky were one. Some might say he was alone - and he was - but he did not feel lonely. Tomorrow was the fifth day and he would greet the dawn with a hurrah for the end of an adventure well lived.

He awakened. In the morning light he could see beyond the slowly moving stream. His eyes squinted to be sure he was not being deceived. The high butte with the three deep ravines, which would carry water in the spring like three great waterfalls, was to the northwest. He had gone beyond it! The left stream channel should have been the one for him to follow.

"The day is young. I am young. I will find the right path." Kincade began to backtrack, humming the forgotten tune he had remembered from once sitting with the rocking woman.

Old Indian's camp was still a ridgeline away, but the boy could smell meat turning on a spit, the juices sizzling onto hot coals. Kincade knew how the grizzly must have felt when she smelled the roasting turkey.

Kincade felt jubilation. He had done it... proven to himself and to Old Indian that he had indeed become a man. The aroma of food grew stronger. The boy's exhilaration made him want to run, but once Old Indian's camp came into view, Kincade slowed to a dignified walk. He would play just a little with Old Indian, letting his mentor know that the past five days had been child's play, even though it had taken every bit of skill he had ever learned.

He strolled forward holding the calendar stick aloft. "Were you expecting company for dinner?" he shouted.

"No, but I have made enough for two. Are you hungry?"

"Not very. Berries and nuts are very filling." He dropped the knife, water-sac, and soft robe. "Are you hungry, Old Indian?"

"Not very. Would you like to tell me about your past five days before we eat?"

Kincade laughed. "Don't tease me any more, Old Indian. I am starved for exactly what you are roasting. I couldn't possibly re-count five long days if I don't immediately get my first good meal in all that time."

Swift Raven smiled and pulled the meat from the skewer. "Eat away. But save a few bites for Old Indian. Your stories can wait."

Actually Swift Raven knew every one of them. Kincade's experiences were also his own. After leaving the blindfolded Kincade he had tied the jaw-thongs of the horses together and given his horse a swat on the rump, knowing that the animals would race back to the campsite. He then brushed away any signs of their departure and signaled Kincade with a wolf call to remove the blindfold. He had clandestinely followed Kincade, never leaving the boy out of his sight just in case there was any life-threatening situation. He almost ruined Kincade's life-lesson when the grizzly appeared. Swift Raven's bow and several arrows had been ready should the animal have turned vicious.

Swift Raven had followed until Kincade took the right fork of the river – the wrong fork. He was confident that the boy would soon find he'd made a mistake and backtrack. This delay would give Swift Raven time to return to the campsite and prepare a good meal that would be greatly appreciated. These five days had proved Kincade was resourceful, self-confident, brave, alone but never lonely - ready to continue on his own in case Sky Fire ever carried out his threat. Old Indian felt proud... enormously and completely proud of the boy who had become his son.

Kincade wiped the juice from his lower lip and licked his fingers. "I am more than satisfied, Old Indian. Now I shall tell you about the most incredible days of my life. Are you ready for a long evening of story telling?"

"I have awaited your return with anticipation. Start at the beginning and leave out nothing." He crossed his legs and handed Kincade a small pipe. "But first let us smoke together for then only the truth can be told."

He lit the bowl and passed it to Kincade. "You first."

CHAPTER 37

SWIFT RAVEN KNEW he was in the autumn of his life. His aching bones had caught up with his aged face.

When he taught Kincade to swim he didn't challenge him to a water fight as he might once have done. When he showed the boy how to catch fish and frogs with his bare hands, he stood on the bank and sang out instructions to Kincade who was knee deep in the stream. Kincade went alone to hunt for deer, coyote, antelope, small elk and moose calves. Then he alone would harvest the kill. Kincade assumed that he was being given tasks to learn from his mentor, not that Swift Raven was no longer capable.

Kincade was fourteen when Swift Raven talked incessantly about hiding. Should Sky Fire find and kill him, the boy should know how to escape.

"Old Indian, is someone chasing us that we must hide?"

The answer did not come easily, for Swift Raven had never explained to Kincade the reason for their constant moving around. Perhaps the boy thought that all boys and their grandfathers did this. Old Indian answered this question. "Let us hope that if we are being chased we can move faster or be smarter than the pursuer.

"Now listen and remember. If there are big boulders to hide among, cover yourself with the brown robe, bunching it over you so that you will look like another rock from a distance.

"If you choose a spot in the woods, do not move for a spooked animal or startled bird could give you away. Watch where your shadow falls and do not let it show where you hide."

Once Swift Raven sought out a beaver pond. Bringing Kincade to the water's edge, he pointed to a large mound of mud and sticks. He said, "Swim underwater until you find the entrance to that mud dome in the center of the pool. It is the lodge of the beaver."

"What do I do when I find it?"

"Swim through the underwater entrance and into the lodge. Raise your head up into the air held within the dome. There will be a ledge where the beaver would sleep. Lie down on it and rest."

"You aren't coming with me?"

"No, it is a small ledge." He knew his breath would fail him swimming under the surface.

"But Old Indian, what if the beaver is sleeping on the ledge and bites me when he wakes up and finds me there?"

"This is an old, deserted lodge. If the beaver lived there, fresh mud would have been packed over the outside. Now go swim and remember if someone is chasing you, this would be a good place to hide."

Kincade prepared to enter the water. Swift Raven said with a slight smile, "Oh, don't rest on the ledge too long. I am getting hungry."

Hiding – why always hiding? Kincade wondered as he disappeared under the water, knowing that the answer would come when it was ready to appear. "Always The Wait," he told himself. "Always...."

During their gathering forays for the cold season, Swift Raven seemed more interested in finding medicinal herbs than berries. For the first time he taught Kincade to identify and collect roots and leaves, pods and seeds which he would boil into a bitter drink or pound into a powder which could be stored.

Kincade had never been around ill people. He had never felt sick himself except once when he had overeaten green crabapples. He wondered about these new preparations which Old Indian ingested daily or kept in a dry place. How could he know unless Old Indian explained without being asked? His response would be the same as so many times before: "Wait and all questions will be answered. You must learn The Wait. That is the Indian Way."

Swift Raven lay on his robe during the cold months, seldom rising to even eat. He would say, "Tell me a story so I will not think of less pleasant things." Kincade recounted as many of the old legends that he could remember. With greater frequency, Swift Raven seemed to drift into the mysterious world where his Recognizable Spirit dwelt.

As time passed, Swift Raven listened to his own Familiar Voice. This Voice had always told him what to do – never what not to do – and it was now telling Swift Raven that soon, the Great Spirit would call for him.

Swift Raven kept the message of the Familiar Voice from Kincade. For now, he would hide the fact that his cough rattled the bones in his chest. He would not tell Kincade that his spittle was laced with blood. But when the warm months came, there would be no hiding from the Great Spirit. Swift Raven knew his time on the earth was coming to its end.

246 Michael Chandler & Loahna Chandler

One morning, Swift Raven knew the time had come to talk with Kincade about death. It would be a new lesson, one that would prepare Kincade for the inevitable. He did not want to frighten the boy, as death was as natural and as glorious as birth. Still, he couched his words in gentle terms.

"Come here," said Old Indian one evening as the two sat across from one another before the fire. "It is time to tell you another belief of my people." Kincade came closer, sitting next to Swift Raven on his buffalo robe. He hoped Old Indian was at last going to answer the unasked questions.

Swift Raven looked directly into Kincade's eyes as the firelight danced across his craggy face. "Death and the afterlife hold no special terror for Indians. I have courted death openly during countless battles. Most Indians believe that a warrior's death is preferable to dying of old age or disease, but that is not to be my choice." He coughed, coughed again, and coughed yet another time.

"May I prepare you a warm drink with herbs, Old Indian?"

He shook his head. "The cough will pass. Give me a moment." Kincade waited in silence and then Swift Raven continued.

"Indians believe that humans and nature are one. There is no clear distinction between the natural and the supernatural. We have come from the Wakan Tanka at birth, and we return to the Wakan Tanka at death."

Kincade looked puzzled. "What is the Wakan Tanka?"

"Wakan Tanka created the universe – it is the universe. It is the seven directions, and the sun, the moon, the stars, the earth, the very rocks, every animal and bird, and creature of the waters." He drew a deep breath as if he were seeing it all before him. "And Kincade, Wakan Tanka is the human soul. It has always been and always will be." He closed his eyes as if he felt peace and comfort in saying the words.

Kincade had listened carefully but did not feel the same comfort. He was afraid to discover what Old Indian was really trying to tell him.

Swift Raven looked into the boy's eyes as if answering this fear. "The spirits of dead loved ones are one with the Wakan Tanka and therefore are everywhere and in everything." He took both of Kincade's hands. "My throat is quite dry after so much talk. Make the warm drink with borage root for both of us and afterwards we will smoke a short pipe together."

Kincade felt a new warmth with the soothing drink and the fragrant smell of the pipe smoke. He would remember this night forever. Old Indian spoke to him and smoked with him as if he were a grown man – a real Indian man.

Gradually the days lengthened and Swift Raven managed to go outside and sit on his robe in the sunshine. He ate more and smiled more and even laughed as Kincade performed tricks on the horse Lightning.

One morning, Kincade awoke to find Old Indian gone. It startled him so that he bolted from his robe and raced outside. There, Old Indian knelt quietly before a clump of black feathers lying just outside the tepee flap.

The messenger raven was dead.

Swift Raven picked it up and stroked its midnight plumage. "You served me well," was all he said. He went inside and found a square of red cloth and wrapped the bird in the ceremonial cover. "We must build a funeral platform, Kincade. Help me to give this loyal scout a final blessing."

With great care and respect, the two erected a small platform on the branches of a tree. There, they gently laid the raven in his red robe, a ceremony that had been repeated over countless centuries for spirits gone to Wakan Tanka.

CHAPTER 38

ABRUPTLY SWIFT RAVEN said, "We go, Kincade."

The boy was startled. It wasn't that his companion never made sudden decisions, but they usually happened when the raven told him it was time to move. Now the raven was wrapped in the red cloth. Did the bird speak from the dead? No matter, such decisions were not to be questioned.

"Do I strike the tepee?"

"No."

"Do I hitch the drags to both horses and load our belongings?"

Swift Raven walked up to Kincade, raised his rough hands to cradle the boy's face, and looked deeply into Kincade's eyes without speaking. Finally, in a soft voice, Old Indian said, "No my son. It is time... We just go."

Swift Raven went into the tepee. When he came out he was putting a leather thong over his head. Attached to it was a small pouch. Once he secured the thin latigo strap around his neck, he dropped the pouch into his shirt. Kincade thought it odd. For as long as he could remember, he had never seen Swift Raven possess anything like the little pouch. It disappeared behind Old Indian's shirt so quickly, that Kincade wondered if he had imagined it.

"Bring my horse." With some effort Swift Raven mounted, but once settled he sat proudly. "Prepare some food for our journey." Kincade did as he was told, and although his curiosity was peaked his voice was silent.

"You follow me." Swift Raven was far down the trail before Kincade caught Lightning and jumped on his back, pressing the horse with his knees in order to catch up.

Over a great many years, Kincade and Swift Raven had covered much ground together. The boy had become familiar with vast areas of land. But this day, Old Indian rode in a new direction, into country Kincade had never seen before.

Morning ended and still they rode on without speaking. Kincade's stomach was reminding him that it had been a long time since he ate a light meal after placing the raven on the platform. He wanted to reach for the pemmican in the pouch tied to Lightning's neck. But why should he eat if Old Indian did not ask for food? He would practice The Wait.

The sun transgressed the highest point in the sky. Swift Raven remained silent, sitting very straight, not looking to right or left, let alone behind where Kincade trotted after him. They moved through the forest, down the foothills and onto the plains.

Kincade began to see something in the distance. It spread out like a herd of buffalo, but it didn't move. As they got closer he remembered once when they looked down on a circle of tepees and Old Indian had called it a village. But there were no tepees and no circle.

Old Indian moved out of the grasses and onto a trail.   It suddenly struck Kincade he had seen this trail, or at least something like it, during the five days he had been tested by Old Indian. There were the same two hard-packed dirt paths running parallel. Each was bordered by tall grass, and in between was short grass with little rocks.

Suddenly two horses were coming very fast down the trail right at Kincade and Old Indian. They were pulling a large flat thing with a man sitting high at one end. He yelled something as he got closer. "Hey, watch out, you dumb Indians!"

"What did he say?" Kincade called to Old Indian, but evidently he wasn't heard.

Kincade jerked Lightning into the tall grass as he and Old Indian were forced to make way for the horses racing past. Kincade stared at four wheels on each corner of the flat thing. He had seen a wheel as big as these during his journey alone. These wheels were spinning very fast. Snapping the jaw-thongs of the two horses was a man whose chin was covered with hair! Kincade's eyes went wide. Hair on a face! On top of a head, yes, but on a face?

The man yelled again as he passed them. "Stay off the road, Redskins!" Again Kincade didn't understand what he said but he seemed angry.

Dust swirled up from the wheels and the horses' hooves, filling Kincade's eyes. The boy cleared his vision with his hands and rode to catch up with Old Indian who had continued on the trail. They were now on the edge of what must be a village, but unlike anything Kincade had ever seen. The dwellings were not made of buffalo hide, but of sliced trees all stuck together to form walls, and the same wood lay flat on the tops.   These big structures were not in a circle but lined up in straight rows with smaller paths between.

Their horses walked into a place filled with people wearing

strange clothes. More men had hair on their faces and sometimes it came down to their chests. Unconsciously Kincade stroked the fuzz on his own chin and upper lip. The women wore puffy coverings on their heads with bills like a duck sticking out over their eyes.

The smells were unlike any he had ever experienced. Not of the forest or stream, but of things burning, of spoiled meat and of sweat. The odors made Kincade's nose wrinkle, but the boy was so fascinated at what surrounded him, it didn't matter.

People stared at him as they rode by. Kincade's eyes were as wide as theirs, for he had never seen human beings with skin this color. It was like dirty snow. Then, as though struck by a thunderbolt, Kincade realized that some of his own skin color matched that of the strange people around him. Though most of his body had been darkened by years of exposure to the sun, there were other pale places - his inner thighs, his arm pits, his belly under the loincloth. He was like them!

Kincade nudged his horse close to Swift Raven's, pulling alongside. "What is this place?"

"It is called a town. White people live here." Swift Raven stopped his horse in front of one of the structures and slid off his horse. "You wait here." He walked up some wooden steps and through a door that swung shut behind him. Kincade did as he was told, looking around with fascination at the different things surrounding him.

Swift Raven had entered a General Store where a half dozen customers drew back at the sight of a savage – however old he was. In sign language that he had long ago forgotten, Swift Raven tried to make the owner understand what he wanted.

The man scratched his head and finally called to the back of the room, "Hey, White Paw Willie, come here and give me a hand understanding this Redskin." A dirty old-timer aimed his chaw at a brass spittoon but missed as he shuffled towards the counter.

"What you want, Savage?" he asked in Swift Raven's language.

"Are you the one who came with soldiers looking for two White boys in my village many seasons ago?"

"Yeah, I remember doin' that. But we only got one. So what?"

"I have the other White boy. He is outside on the horse."

"What's he sayin', White Paw?" the owner asked.

"He's got a kid that me and the army went huntin' years ago. Hell, I'd almost forgot about that." He then turned back to ask, "So what? You want somethin'?"

Swift Raven did not like the looks or the smell of this man but there was no one else. "The soldiers offered a reward for his return. I return him and I want a reward."

White Paw Willie burst out laughing. "Damn thieving bastard wants to swap the kid for gold!" he said to those in the store.

"Ask him how much gold," one old sourdough shot back. "Maybe the Army will pay us the reward instead of him."

White Paw Willie spit again making no attempt to come even close to the spittoon. "How much gold?" he asked.

Swift Raven shook his head and whispered, "No gold. A good rifle and a jug of whiskey."

Willie's guffaw was loud and raucous. "They's all alike, these Redskins! He just wants a gun and a jug of rot-gut. What ya' think, Slim?" he asked the store owner. "You wanna make a trade?"

Both men went to the front window and looked at Kincade who sat waiting. "Guess I can find those two things, but he better not ask for nothin' else or he can take the boy back to his tepee."

White Paw Willie explained to Old Indian that the trade was okay but he would have to wait while the store owner found a rifle and a jug. Swift Raven went to the window and stared at the boy on the horse... his boy. Old Indian's legs began to buckle and his shoulders shook at the ache he felt deep inside. Nothing in his entire life had ever hurt so much. A chill crawled into his heart so he stepped away from the window. To show his feelings would not be the Indian Way.

Kincade sat on Lightning and waited. It was a hot day and he pulled off his buckskin shirt, folding it in front of him. A boy about his own age had been walking around and around the horse staring at Kincade.

"Hey you, up there," the circling boy finally shouted. "What's your name?" Kincade didn't answer. "I said what's your name... your name? Don't you speak English?"

Kincade vaguely remembered some words that had served him well a long time ago. "I Kincade." He pointed to his chest. "Kincade."

"That's a pretty dumb name. Kincade! Never heard such a dumb name before." He began throwing small rocks at Lightning's rump and the animal became skittish. Kincade tried to calm the horse with stroking and the gentle Indian words he always used.

"You know that old Redskin is tryin' to sell you? The highest bid so far is a rusty rifle and some firewater."

Kincade wondered to himself, "What's this boy talking about?" But he said nothing and practiced The Wait until Swift Raven came out of the building with a gun and a jug.

"What's happening?" Kincade asked him.

Swift Raven put the jug in a bag slung around the neck of his horse. "These are not for me. They are for a powerful brave of my tribe. He is the one who has been hunting us. I will not give you back to him. But I will bring him these presents – a good horse, a good gun, a good jug of whiskey. He will think it a good trade and he will let me stay in my village again."

He slung the rifle strap across his shoulder. "Put on your shirt. Get off your horse." Kincade did what he was told, still not believing what was happening.

Stepping close to the boy so no one could see his actions, Swift Raven took a medicine bag from around his neck and handed it to Kincade. The outside of the pouch had pretty beads of various colors, formed in a circle. "Put it around your neck," he whispered. "Keep it inside your shirt. Show it to no one. It has my secret on the outside – your secret on the inside."

"My secret, Old Indian?" Kincade asked but there was no answer.

Swift Raven took the jaw-thong of Kincade's horse Lightning, and lightly sprang onto his own as if not wanting to appear decrepit in front of the Whites. "You will live here now. I go back to my tribe and you come back to yours. I will die soon but you will not watch me."

Kincade could see great pain in Old Indian's eyes, but it wasn't from his body hurting. This pain was racking the old man's heart.

No further words were shared. Old Indian – the only person Kincade had ever really known – left the boy standing in the dusty street with the bully laughing and pointing at him.

(Continued in the novel "KINCADE'S BLOOD")

EPILOGUE

S WIFT RAVEN NO longer thought of himself as Old Indian. It had been the boy's name for him and that part of his life was over. He did not return to their last campsite to retrieve the tepee or his belongings. He might cry, and even though no one would be there to see him, it was not the Indian Way to show grief – to feel it, yes, but not show it - even to himself. Slowly he made his way back to the tribe he and Kincade had left over ten years before.

When he arrived, riding his own horse and leading Lightning on a rope, he saw smoke rising from the largest tepee where the head-men and councillors gathered. He gave the jaw-thongs to a young boy and stood at the entrance until his presence was recognized.

"I am Kangee Kohana, once a loyal scout for your people. May I enter?"

"We know who you are, ancient one," the Chief said, then paused for what seemed a time as he looked into Kangee Kohana's eyes. Finally, the Chief spoke once more. "We welcome you back after a long absence. Come, be among us." He entered and stood humbly before men he had once known as friends.

"Sit and we will smoke a pipe in honor of your safe return."

A place was made for the old man and fresh leaves packed into the bowl of a long pipe. A spark was taken from the central fire and fragrance filled the tepee.

"Will you recount your years, Kangee Kohana, so that we may know more of your life away from us?"

Swift Raven spoke of many adventures, but never mentioned Kincade. The pipe had passed to every man and all had listened with rapt attention. "Have you returned to spend your final days with us?" the Chief asked.

"No, I come to ask a question. I am looking for a man who was once a brave warrior and hunter in our tribe. His name is Mahpee Paytah. Do any of you know where I can find him?"

On hearing Sky Fire's name, the headmen and councillors looked to one another, but none spoke as if it was up to the Chief to answer this question.

He placed the pipe at the edge of the center fire and was silent for a few moments with his head bowed as if thinking. "Why do you wish to find him?"

"I wish to make peace with him. I bring him gifts."

The Chief rose. "Then I shall take you to him." He led the way from the tepee and walked toward the edge of the village. Here, outside the main circle, lived those who were infirmed, either by age or health. They were tended by old crones and were dependent for all their needs on the charity of the tribe.

Swift Raven looked at the unkempt area. "He lives here?" The Chief nodded. "What happened to make him fall into such conditions? When I was part of this tribe he was the greatest among us."

The Chief stopped and again looked into the old man's eyes. "Many seasons ago he came back to us, being dragged by his faithful horse. In a moment you will see why he stays."

The Chief turned and they resumed their walk, approaching a small six-skin tepee with a neglected, black horse tied to a stake. Its once proud head was drooping and its tail swished flies that buzzed around its sweat. Sitting in the dirt was Sky Fire, a jug resting at his side. His bare arms, once so straight and strong, were bent like twigs broken for kindling. His crossed legs were too crippled to support his body. He stared at the two watching him. Recognizing neither, he lifted the jug and took a long drag which ran down his lips to his chin.

Swift Raven turned to the Chief. "Has he no family, no friends to rescue him from this degradation?"

The Chief shook his head. "The only one who shows any interest is a scout from our neighboring village. In fact you know him. He is Ozuye Najin, married to your two daughters. He frequently brings Mahpee Paytah a jug of the White man's firewater which seems to give him relief from the pain in his limbs."

"I shall return to find my horse, for I too bring him relief from that which has pained him - not in his limbs but in his spirit."

The Chief nodded in understanding. "You will be welcome if you wish to stay with us."

The old man replied, "No, but your friendship will always be returned."

Swift Raven got the jug and the rifle from his horse but left both animals with the boy as he returned to the tepee of Sky Fire. He knelt before his old nemesis and looked into his bleary eyes.

"I am Kangee Kohana," he began. He saw no reaction. "You

have ruined your life in order to kill me, but I am still here. I was never running because I was afraid you would find me. I was only using you as an excuse to play a game of hide-and-seek with the son I never fathered. I had him for many, many years and taught him the Indian Way. Now the game is over and I no longer need you."

He placed the new jug next to the old one. "Live on in your oblivion." He put the rifle into the shaking hands. "Clutch your dreams of vengeance. They are as empty of harm as this gun is empty of bullets." Not a word had been heard as Sky Fire drank again from the old jug of whiskey. Swift Raven retrieved both horses and rode away.

His final days were spent living in the large tepee of his two daughters, Pretty Butterfly and Laughing Maiden. There was always good talk with their husband, scout Standing Warrior and the tribe's chief, Brave Eagle. His greatest joy was watching the little children of the village who called him Tunkasila - Grandfather.

One moonless and very quiet night, as the starlight bathed the village, Kangee Kohana left this world to join the Wakan Tanka. With his last breath, a kind smile appeared on his withered face.

For as the old man crossed over, his heart filled with the memories of the young boy he loved more than life itself: His son, Kincade.

THE END

"Complete your...

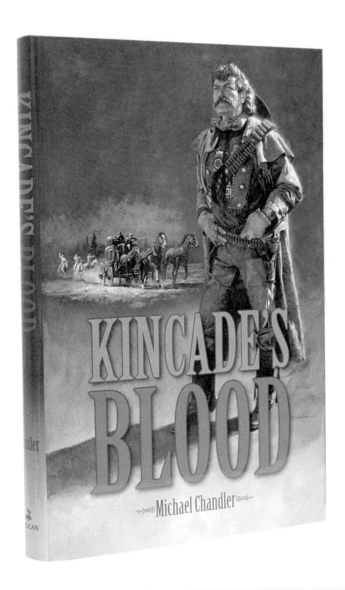

...Kincade adventures"

"The heart-pounding sequel to Kincade's Blood!"

KINCADE'S FEAR

Michael Chandler & Loahna Chandler